Masama

Masama

Or

The Adventures of
Twing and Twang

Rainer Neumann

Published by

Second Edition

Published by *landseandsky* in 2007

ISBN: 978 0 6151-6009-2

Cover art is a watercolor painting by the author.

This book is available through the electronic storefront of
lulu.com/Rneumann.

Inquiries are also welcomed at highwayone@earthlink.net

To the boys who first laughed
at Twing and Twang
and Sheriff O'Malley
and the Browser
during that vacation near
Masama.

Prologue

Why, you may ask would such an alliteration of sounds such as Twing and Twang ever grace the pages of a manuscript and be worthy of a story that you could read or hear or imagine. It is a valid question because twing twang could easily be taken for an old pop song, at least the beginnings of one or a strum on the strings of a country guitar, twing, twang, twing, twaaaaang or just a whimsical romp in an idyllic countryside with two unlikely twin brothers meeting the likes of the Browser and his friend Mouse and Sheriff O'Malley and, and, and Angelina. She comes late in the story as do all of those characters. It's Twing and Twang that need to be fleshed out first and they have very different upbringings. Oh, just a note before we get into Twing's life, the main title of this adventure, 'Masama' is the name of a real place in the state of Washington, a sort of outpost for vacations or . . . adventure.

Twing

You see, Twing and his twin brother Twang had not seen each other in 18 years and it could be said that they had never seen each other. Twing was made aware of this possibility but could not quite believe that it was true. Twang had no idea. They are going to meet near Masama, which is in the Methow River Valley on the eastern side of the Cascade Mountains. It was to be their meeting place because of a letter Twing had received from two people he had never seen before.

The letter came to Twing just after he graduated from high school in Boulder Creek, California. It seemed like his life was just beginning when the letter came. He read it and then he had to read it again:

> To the 18 year old Twing:
> When you read this be prepared for a shock. Sit down. You have a twin brother. You were taken away right after you were

born. Strange events made it difficult for you to grow up together. After all these years I feel that you should know this. You were adopted and brought to America. Your brother was brought up in another country. He has recently taken a trip to the United States. You may find him in the state of Washington in the vicinity of a place called Masama. That is all I can tell you. I was sworn to secrecy many years ago but I feel that the time has come for you to find out about your true past.

Sincerely,

A loyal friend of your true father

Twing had just started working in the Coffee Cantata when this letter was given to him by a man dressed in a worn out yet well-kept tweed jacket. He was not from Boulder Creek and his companion seemed excited when the man talked to Twing. The man had noticed a birthmark on Twing's neck and he had asked him about it. Twing was a little embarrassed about this. He usually hid this blemish so it wouldn't be noticed but this morning he was in a hurry and simply grabbed a T-shirt. It was not a large birthmark but it did have an unusual shape, like that of a guitar. It almost looked like a tattoo until you looked closer. The man asked Twing how long he had lived here and what his name was. Twing told him his real name was Twingly Birdwell but everyone called him Twing or . . . He decided not to tell them his other name. At that the couple started to talk to each other in excited yet hushed voices. Before he saw them again they had left the cafe and on their table was an envelope with his name on it.

To: TWING, it said on the outside in large letters. Next to it was a 50-dollar bill. He took the letter and the bill and ran out of the cafe to find them. "They must have made a mistake with the tip," he thought. He looked around but he did not see them. He only heard the sound of a car roaring north on Highway 9. He stood there for a minute until someone called, "Twing I need a latte." Twing jerked up and went back inside. After work he was able to open the envelope. Inside was the letter that started his adventures with his unknown twin brother.

He had much to tell his mom when he came home that evening and much to ask. "I got a letter today, mom. It said I was adopted. It said I have a twin brother somewhere. It said . . . Well, here, you read it." She stood silently for a long while. She didn't even want to take the letter. "Mom," he said "what's up? What's going on? Was I adopted? Do I have a twin brother?"

"I don't know about a twin brother," she simply acknowledged. "I don't know about a brother at all," she emphasized, trying to avoid further conversation and the subject of adoption.

"But how could I have a twin brother if you don't know about it?" he insisted.

"Twing," she sighed, "I guess, I guess it's inevitable that you would find out someday. I just couldn't tell you yet."

"What?" he asked, "Tell me what?"

"Years ago, your father and I were told we couldn't have any children so we talked about adopting a child. At that time your father was with an international company in England. He knew someone or his boss knew someone who was giving up a child for adoption. They made all the arrangements and we ended up with a baby boy. I never heard about a twin brother. Not too long after you came to us your father had a chance to move to Boulder Creek and set up his own business. We were just getting started when your father died. You were four and a half years old. When you turned five I sold the business and bought this house. You went to school and I went to work and we both ended up taking care of each other. I don't know what this letter means. I just don't want you to leave . . ."

"But mom I've got to find out what this is all about.

4

I've got to find my brother, to see if he is alive and what happened to him. You'll always be my mom, but why did they, those two, leave an envelope. Why didn't they just tell me? Why did they leave like that? I've got to find out. I've got to figure this out. I'm going to go to Masama."

His mother knew she wasn't going to be able to stop him. He had a stubborn streak in him that had helped him through school and gotten him a black belt in Aikido. The only black belt in Boulder Creek. "Aikido is not just a martial art" he had told her often enough, "it is a physical and mental philosophy."

But all she knew was that he went out carrying his gray workout suit and one day she saw him with a black belt around his waist.

He gave notice at the Cafe Cantata and thought about how he would take on this quest. Realizing he would have to leave his souped-up Maverick with his mom he made reservations with United Airlines to fly out of the San Jose airport. Somehow he felt this was a path he had to take. Somehow, with this letter, his life had taken on a new meaning. His mother felt it and dreaded it at the same time. She had lived her life for him and now he wasn't even her son. No matter how much he reassured her, she knew things were different.

When it was time she drove him to the airport. As he

was saying good-bye she gave him a small pouch his father had left him, which she had promised to give to him when he turned 18. He put it in his pocket, gave his mother one last hug and headed for Gate 6.

When that 747 left the ground it was as if all the years of anticipation were in the takeoff. He was on his own for the first time in his young life. For the first-time he also felt a bittersweet feeling welling up inside of him. He was also leaving his mother. "She would always be his mother to him," he thought, "no matter what he would find out about his birth mother." As the plane flew higher he thought about her and the father he had lost so long ago, at least the man he thought was his father. Even now he still had some memories of him or maybe stories that had become memories. "All these years I have been going further and further away from you," he thought, and now, away from mom, from home," He felt like he was going out of an atmosphere of security, into his own orbit, like a rocket blasting off. He couldn't help but think of a song, or at least his version of an old pop song,

> Rocket man, I'm going into space now.
> Rocket man, I'm going to find my place
> now. ah ah ah . . .

He kept singing it over and over, adding his own words,

until the clouds covered the earth, until they did not seem like clouds anymore. It looked like a barren cold snow-covered land, as if one were traveling over the Antarctic. "This must be what it looks like," he thought "a wonderful cotton-light world." He wanted to jump into it, he wanted to lie in it, but something reminded him that things were not always what they seemed. Even his seat belt reminded him that he had something else in his pocket, the pouch his mother had given him. He took it out, pulled on the string, opened it up and dropped a ring on his open palm. He looked at it and put it on his ring finger. It fit perfectly.

"What a beauty," the words whistled out.

He landed in Seattle at SeaTac. Now to get his pack and find a bus to the Amtrak station. He was going to take a train to Wenatchee, from there he would hitchhike up to Mazama.

Everything looked new to him. He felt a bounce in his step. Every face seemed to have a whole world behind it. He looked around for bus information and finally asked at an information booth. There was a local bus that went to downtown Seattle. The Amtrak station was not too far away.

Seattle, the rainy city, was overcast but he rode as if the sun streamed through his window. There was the space needle. "Wow!" he said, too loudly because several people turned their heads including a cute girl across the aisle from him. His stop came up and he breathed the air of the harbor. Huge car ferries were on the water. He had just enough time to walk through the fish market. There were glistening salmon, there were vendors wanting to get your attention, there was blueberry jam, even blueberry salsa and the aroma of coffee being roasted somewhere. He tried an espresso, which they seemed to sell on every corner. He had gotten used to drinking a latte occasionally but today it was going to be a shot of espresso, maybe a double.

He noticed the time and realized he had "bummeled" long enough. That was a word his German teacher taught him to describe a slow stroll through the market or the town or where ever and it seemed very appropriate at this moment.

He finally reached the Amtrak station. It was being renovated to its past glory. The false ceilings were being taken out and he could see through a skylight area to the original carved ceilings. "This is going to look good," he thought, "Now why would they want to cover up that original ceiling? Was it just something people had to do, just to change things?" As he got in line for a ticket an agent came by and gave him all the information. The train to Wenatchee was on track 8 and getting ready to go in a few minutes. Twing also asked him about train service to Masama but Amtrak had no rail line going north from Wenatchee. He would have to take a Greyhound from there and he could catch one right from the train station. "That's pretty good service," he said to the short man with the camouflaged pants behind him. The man just nodded but Twing felt an excitement in all of this, more so than at the airport. There, it was too packaged. There, he felt like he was herded into a small seat and had no choice. Here, he felt like a part of the history of the West with more room to stretch out and take in the whole country.

The train left Seattle in the year of '82'. "Hey, that sounds like an old song, (he had a penchant for putting new words on old pop songs). "East from Seattle, go east to find your own," he sang silently. He felt like intoning the sounds. Sea attle. Sea, from the sea, the sound of the sea, Chief Seattle. On to Wenatchee. Another Indian name, Wen nat she. "What does it mean?" he wondered as he sank into the comfort of his window seat. With the rhythm of the wheels he drifted off to sleep.

"Twing, another latte." "Coming, coming." He rushed out with the fancy brew only to find himself on a high mountain. This one had a fire lookout on it. "Here you go." He gave it to the firewatcher. "That's what I like about this job," the fire watcher said, "all the comforts, and a great view." Twing was aghast at what he saw. The peaks of many mountains around him. Inside the tower was a round table with the name of the peaks on it. He especially like the wine peaks—Burgundy, Merlot, Pinot and Cabernet. All red wines. "This will keep the valley healthy," he thought. "A strike! A strike!" The firewatcher pointed to a lower hill where lightning had struck. He called into the wireless radio telling the fire department where he had seen it.

"That's what I like about my job. The lightning. That's why they call me 'Lightning Bill'." The clouds moved fast over them. "Looks like we're in for it," Lightning Bill said. "You're going to have to stay here. It's not safe to go down now. We may be in for a few jolts." The first one that struck rattled Twing's teeth as it traveled down the lightning rod. The whole room was lit up in a wild spectacle. This was raw power. It was as close as he ever got to the power of Zeus. The power of the gods. "Remember me," Zeus was saying. "I am the power of the heavens. The lightning throne."

Another bolt shook the hut and set his hair on end. Another hit and he felt over come by the awesome power. "If he lived through this he would, he would . . ."

He was shaken by the conductor. "Your ticket." He looked around, a conductor wanted his ticket. Where had he been?

"Ticket please." He fumbled around in his pocket and gave him the ticket to Wenatchee. "Thank you." The conductor stuck the ticket on the overhead compartment and walked on. Another person asked if he wanted to make reservations for dinner in the dining car. "Sure, when?" "6:30 is open." "Okay, I'll be there."

Needing to go to the bathroom he went down the stairs of the rail car. When he looked into the mirror he was shocked to see his hair standing on end. "What! They must have thought I was nuts up there." He looked again and started chuckling. "Looks pretty good," he thought. "Twing, the lightning rod. Maybe I could start a new trend."

He left it up and went in search of the dining car. What a ride. Careening down the aisle he noticed other passengers making themselves at home in their seated areas. In between the cars it was a jerky ride but the dining car seemed an island of tranquility. He was seated with a family of three. "What a ride," he said to them. The little girl stared at his hair. She finally ventured to ask, "What happened to your hair?" "Oh, I was hit by lightning," he told her. She laughed, but wasn't sure whether to believe him. He ordered the fried chicken with mashed potatoes. He had a real tablecloth and silverware. "Wow! They do this all right."

"We're going into a tunnel," the little girl said, "hold

your breath." He tried but soon gave up. When they came out, he noticed the country around them had changed. Rising cliffs were on both sides of the train. He could not see the top. A river flowed next to them, glistening through the fir trees. "This is country," he thought. "Wow! Yea. Look, a trestle. We're going over a trestle," he said to the little girl.

When he finally got back to his seat, he noticed a package with a note around it. "Twangly" is all it said. That's funny, they spelled my name wrong. Is this a present from Amtrak or what? Nobody else knows I'm here. He opened and found a small tape recorder. He was taken by surprise. It's not from Amtrak. Then, who else knows he's on this train? My mother? She sent me a package? Can't be. They must still be on the train? That is, unless they got off at the last stop. "Wow!" he said. He put on the earphones and pressed play. A kind of flute music came on. "Nothing from around here," he thought. It was like Middle Eastern or Asian music. Then a voice came on:

> You have escaped from your father's sanctuary.
> You cannot escape from the revolutionary guards.
> This will be the end of your line.

"This is strange," he thought. He began to rewind the tape. At the same time he started to look around. Everybody seemed to have settled in. A child kept wanting to play peek-a-boo with him. The mother kept urging her back. He decided to walk through the cars. Holding the tape recorder he looked left and right but didn't see anyone who seemed strange to him or who seemed to be focusing on him. Several people were covered with blankets but who was he looking for. It could have been anyone. Now this trip was taking on an added dimension. Suddenly, there seemed to be two different sides to his journey. One was urging him on, the other had added a confusing doomsday message. When he got back to his seat he played the tape again. The music came on. Now the words, the voice, the same message was heard:

> You have escaped from your father's sanctuary.
> You cannot escape from the revolutionary guards.
> This will be the end of your line.

Was he imagining things? It was a strange accent. The warning had repeated. Was this for him? He sat back and let the rest of the tape play. Music. As he thought about his journey, a feeling welled up inside of him. He felt a drive to go on, to find out what was happening. He finally realized that he had to find his brother. It was like going into his past, in order to go into the future. Who was going to stop him? This just made his resolve stronger. He made a silent vow: "Twingly Birdwell is going to find out where he came from. He's going to find his brother, if he has one! No matter what."

The high cliffs outside his windows seemed to coincide with his strong will and he was filled with a sense of destiny. "That was Snoqualmie Pass," someone announced over the intercom speakers. "We are now beginning our descent into the Columbia River Valley. We'll be in Wenatchee in approximately 90 minutes." The firs and pines began to thin out and the hills were becoming rounder and dryer with sagebrush over sagebrush brown. Along the river were orchards, sometimes going up into the hills. This is apple country, orchards and orchards irrigated by the river. I read about the great Columbia. I heard Woody Guthrie sing its praises, "Roll on Columbia", and it rolled until they built the massive Grand Coulee dam. They tamed that mighty river so that apple's could grow and houses could glow with the electricity from its generators." He had studied the Columbia River history and heard about the pioneers traveling into Oregon and Washington not so many years ago. "Roll on Columbia, roll on Twingly," he thought.

"Wenatchee, next stop, Wenatchee." He hurried down the stairs to get his backpack. As he went down he thought about his situation. "Wait a minute. Whoever knows I'm on this train will probably expect me to get off here. I'm going to stay on for one more stop. I hope it's not too far. Then I'll backtrack. I can sleep out somewhere if I have to." He took his backpack and went into the bathroom. Tight fit. I'll wait until the train starts again. "Hah, hah," he chuckled to himself. This is strange but exciting.

The train pulled out. He waited a few minutes, then put his backpack in the rack again. He knew he couldn't sit down at his seat because he didn't have a ticket so he stayed in the door area. He could look out and watch the country become flatter and browner. I wonder where the next stop will be. He got out his map. Next stop looks like Ephrata. If the train stops there I'm on my way.

He had not noticed but a woman was standing in the lower car with him, right next to the door. He asked her if she was getting out at Ephrata. "Yes, how about you? Where are you going?" "Oh, I'm getting off also," he answered, "I'm going to travel north from here." "You should have gotten off at Wenatchee. The main highway goes north from there. It's a beautiful highway. It goes along the Columbia River for a while, then turns towards the Cascades along the Methow River. If you take Highway 20 north it will go through a town called Winthrop. I have a good friend there. She has a daughter about your age.

She was rambling on about a mile a minute. Twing couldn't even ask a question she was talking so fast. "What's your name?" "My friends call me Twing," he hesitated but he had answered. He wasn't used to being secretive. "Twing, now, that's an interesting name. You're probably just out of high school. Oh, I loved that time of my life. That was the year I went to Seattle. Can you believe it. To Seattle. Now you don't even think about it at all. How are you going to go?"

"I'm going to hitchhike."

"Hitchhike! Well, be careful who you get in the car with. You look like you could take care of yourself. But I'll give you my friend's name and phone number in Winthrop. Maybe you could stay with her. She has a little farm next just outside of the town. She always needs some help clearing something or picking something."

"Here." She handed him a piece of paper with the name, Mariah West, 313-8888. "Her daughters name is

Angelina."

As he took it he noticed the train had stopped. The doors were being opened. They both stepped out. Oh, the air felt fresh. He shook her hand. She wished him well and said, "My name is Sarah. Tell Mariah that I sent you." He thanked her and stood on the platform while she disappeared. Now he had a chance to look around. No one else had gotten off the train. He watched the train pull away and for the first time he felt alone.

Before he knew it, a car came close to where he was standing. "Twing," someone called. He was blinded by the lights of the car. He held his hands in front of his eyes to shield himself from the light and the car or whatever else might be coming at him. He finally grabbed his pack and, almost out of instinct, stepped into the shadow of the train station.

"Twing, it's Sarah. Get in. I can't leave you in the night like this. You can sleep at my place, then I'll drive you to Wenatchee. I've got to get something there."

His reaction went from cold to warm and he laughed at his momentary fear. By the time he told Sarah that he thought she was going to run him over she had turned into a driveway of a small brick bungalow with a porch and a two-seated swing. "You can sleep on the porch. It'll be cooler out here," she said as she went in the front door. "I'll see you in the morning." Within minutes

Twing was lying in his sleeping bag with a white banister around him. He even saw a shooting star falling in the direction of Masama. I wonder if that's for my brother. Somewhere in that direction is my brother. My brother, "he ain't heavy Lord. He's my brother." But his weariness had overtaken him and the vast sky let him rest.

Twang

As the Washington State night closed in on Twing we take our story even further eastward, over a great continent and across the Atlantic Ocean to a fabled isle. The evening is misty and two friends have just left a Solstice gathering near the river Thames. Along a well-worn bridal path, surrounded by hedges and long moonlight shadows they swagger and sway and talk of the future.

"Wherefore goest thou Twang or should I say whyfor? Why? Why master Twang, do you leave us in such disarray. If you go away what will happen to our play? Master Twang?"

"Oberon, it is not for me to carry the day. Another part will come your way, another part will come your way."

Twang put his arms around his friend and they both laughed at their histrionics. "What a year it has been, eh? We started with Macbeth and we ended up in dreamland. You played the part of the ghost of Banquo and then went to the king of the fairies. I went from Malcolm the son of a king to Puck, the bearer of charms and potions.

"Tell me Rushdie, am I dreaming still?"

"Yes, my friend we have one more performance in the garden of make believe, in the garden of magic and then we disband and go our ways for the summer."

"Which way will you go, Rushdie?" Twang asked him, "Will you go to Oxford in the fall? Have you decided that?"

"I don't know yet. I do have an offer to go but I also have to help my father this summer. Most likely I will be on campus in the fall. My father's business is expanding to America. He's opening a manufacturing plant on the northwest coast of America, just south of Seattle, I think."

"That sounds exciting but it doesn't mean you can't come back this fall. We have to stay in touch. We're lifelong friends."

"We will. In any case, we've made our vows. The New Planet members of Evolution are connected no matter where we are," he said with a sly grin.

"Still it would be a grand adventure, to travel around the world together, wouldn't it?" Twang excitedly asked his friend. "We could get started in Seattle, go to

Vancouver, go south, go east . . . We've got to see the U. S. of A. and the Cascades, the Cascade Mountains. His enthusiasm trailed as he thought of his parents, especially his father's fanatical insistence that he stay in England and not travel outside of England.

"Why don't you come?" His friend insisted. Twang reminded him of his father's situation and yet at the same time wondered himself why he couldn't travel outside of England. "It's strange at this point in my life. I mean I can't stay here forever. I'm going to leave some time or least travel a bit."

"When will you leave?" Twang asked his friend.

"I believe it's the day after our last performance. Think on it, Master Twang. Adieu until tomorrow."

"Adieu and farewell, my king." Twang wandered slowly back to Eton Hall with mixed emotions. His friend's enthusiasm for travel had grabbed him. He could feel the yearning coming over him quite like the shadows that covered his feet, his knees and finally broke over his belly. They seemed to cover him and then let him go as the path opened to a field only to come again. He felt this come over him several times until he was lost in the rhythm of his walk and the movement of the shadows. Suddenly a hand pulled at him. It was the huge hand of his father who spoke sternly, "Twang, don't go in too far. There is an undertow there." He was jolted out of his rhythmic reverie, out of his thoughts, and remembered his father saying that to him when he was eight or nine years old on the rare occasion he went wading in the river. But here and now Twang wanted to stay in that rhythm, that movement, and let the shadows entice him into something unknown.

"If only I could be allowed some more freedom," he thought. "What keeps us all here? I mean why can't we travel abroad like other families I know? It was a question he had asked his father numerous times. He had always gotten the same answer. "Our family business keeps us in England." "Well, what business was that? Anyway, at this time, in this age of global businesses like his friend Rushdie's family business, he could not reconcile his father's stubbornness. "Eventually," he thought, "he would have to find out. Maybe when his parents come up after the last performance would he be able to bring up the subject again." Tonight, he would allow this feeling of adventure overtake him, at least as much as a hot bath could accomplish.

Bye, Bye Sucker

Caw, squack, caw. Crows were making a racket across the street. They were an alarm clock he couldn't shut off. Now the sun streamed through the slats of the porch. They looked like long swords ready to penetrate his sleeping bag. He got up, stretched and looked around this expanse of land. "Big enough for me," he thought, as he breathed in the aroma of sage. "Ahh, man, that smells great."

"Twing," Sarah called out, "Would you like some coffee or orange juice?" "Sounds good." He rolled up his sleeping bag and joined her for breakfast. "We have to leave soon. Before it gets too hot." He packed up his sleeping bag and put his pack in the car. They rolled off in the direction of Wenatchee.

"Apples, apples, apple's," he said as they drove closer to Wenatchee, "What a paradise." "Thanks to the Columbia River," she added. Now I'll drop you off at the junction of Highway 97 and Highway 2. Go north and be careful."

He felt like he'd just been turned in the right direction. His pack by his side, he sat by the highway in the cool morning sun. "How beautiful", he thought. He looked at the hills to the west and the valley to the north. He was going to pull out his map and, instead, said, "This is my new map, the land itself. I've got to get to know the land." He was so caught up in surveying the land that he didn't notice a rundown old Chevy sedan pull up beside him. "You want a ride?" It was a mousy looking kid about his age with a straw cowboy hat on. He was leaning out of the passenger side. Twing looked in to see a large man with a beard behind the wheel. The kid got out and opened the trunk. Twing helped him put his pack inside. He had just taken out his journal and put it into the bag with the tape recorder. The pouch and ring his mother had given him was in his pocket. The kid closed the trunk and hopped in the front door. The back door was still locked as Twing waited for them to open it.

"Bye, bye, sucker," the kid said as the bearded man pressed on the gas. Tires squealed and the car roared off leaving Twing in dust and gravel and dirt. "What! Wait, wait you bastards," he yelled, "Wait, wait! How could you do that. You didn't need to do that. You didn't need to do that. You didn't . . ." His eyes started to well up with tears. He couldn't believe someone would do that. He felt like everything had been taken away from him. How could they. "Oh", he thought, "oh mom, what have I done?"

They had taken off down the highway with his backpack in the trunk. Now he really felt alone and betrayed. Betrayed by people he didn't know and even more, betrayed by his own naiveté. Finally, he sat down, looked around him, opened his journal and started to write:

Monday, the 21st,
"Got taken today. I mean really. I let someone just take off with my things. It looks like I'm going down to nothing before I really start."

"Sounds like a song," he said, "I've got plenty of nothing, nothings plenty for me. I've got my . . ." He looked around. "I've got this journal. I've got my coat. I've got the apple trees. Oh, I've got plenty of nothing. mmm mmm mmm." He began to feel better. "I've got my wits," he thought, "that's what will carry me through. That'll get me there." But he also thought of something else as he looked into the direction he was going, as he looked into the sky. "Did anyone, anyone see this? Is there someone up there who sees these things? Anyone?"

Cars were coming by now. He got up and put his thumb out signaling the next driver. A few cars passed him, an old pickup passed him. He heard a horn and looked around. The pickup had stopped about 50 feet past him. He was elated but also more wary. He had no backpack, he just had himself. He opened the door to the pickup, looked in and saw a weather beaten old farmer. "I, I'm going to Winthrop," Twing said.

"Weeell get in. That's where I'm heading. I've got to get me some bailing wire." Twing jumped in and sat quietly as they headed north next to the almost mighty Columbia. They sat quietly for while. Twing thought the man and old pickup had been hauling hay for years. He must know this country, this land, the river, the seasons.

"What's the weather like on the eastern side of the mountains?" Twing asked.

The old man answered slowly, "well, we don't get as much rain and it gets hot in the summer."

"Looks like you been living around here for while." Twing stated.

"All my life, been helping out here and there, ever since they put in the Grand Coolie Dam."

"What year was that?"

"That was back in 37. Before the war."

"You've probably seen a few changes."

"I've seen a few. Some I like and some I don't like. We've turned sagebrush into orchards and the dam has lit up our farms. We've also had a lot more people move here and a lot more people like, I presume yourself, are traveling through."

"Yeah, I'm going to meet my brother in Masama."

"You're on your way to the mountains then?"

"Well, maybe. I'm not sure. We haven't seen each other in a long time."

They looked out. "We're leaving the Columbia now and going into the Methow valley. That's the Methow River there." He pointed to the left. The valley was beginning to enfold them. "It looks greener here," Twing thought. For the first-time he remembered his home in Boulder Creek surrounded by hills of firs and redwoods. He also thought of his mother, alone and probably worried about him. He'd better call her when he gets to Winthrop.

They drove through Methow and Carlton and Twisp. "Twisp," he thought, "where'd they get a name like that?" He smiled and said, "Twisp, that's about like Twing, which is my name. Twing and Twisp."

"Next stop Winthrop. Where ya going?"

"Oh, I'm going to see someone over there. A Mariah

West. She lives out-of-town somewhere."

"I know Mariah. I'm the godfather of her daughter. I'll drop you off there."

"That's very kind," Twing answered and felt very lucky to have gotten this ride. They drove out and the farmer said, "That's her place down the road. I'll drop you off here. Say hello to her from Jim, Jim Bridger. Tell her I'll stop in soon." Twing got out of the pickup, walked up a dusty road to an old farmhouse. "Needs a little work" he thought. A dog started barking. Twing held up his hands and shouted "hello, anyone?"

"Who is it?" came a voice from inside.

"My name is Twing. A friend of yours, Sarah told me you might have some work to do."

"Well hold on." A woman came out of the front door holding a paintbrush in one hand and wearing a well-painted apron.

"Well, come on in. Looks like you're traveling light."

"There's a reason for that. Two guys took my backpack outside of Wenatchee."

"How did that happen?"

Twing told her the whole story and how he had been given a ride up here by an old farmer named, Jim Bridger.

"Gees, I haven't seen Jim for a week or so. I wish he'd stopped in. Those guys who took your pack were just pure mean. But, listen, I do need some things done around here. Some fence to be fixed, a door problem, etc, etc. The only trouble is I don't have much money at this time. I'm waiting for the "reds" to get ripe. I can put you up and feed you though, at least for a few days."

Twing thanked her and was eager to take up her offer.

"Okay, I'll make of a list of things that need to be done. Meanwhile, you can meet young Shep, our Collie. Come here boy. Meet Twing. Is that right?"

"Yes, it's actually Twingly Birdwell, but everyone calls me Twing.

"Well, I can see why, Twingly Birdwell. That's a strange one. Sounds like a country singer to me. Do they call you anything else?"

"Well, a few kids called me T-bird and that's because I love to work on old cars."

"Well, T-Bird, why don't you take Shep out and let him take you around the place. Make yourself at home."

Twing rubbed Shep's neck and headed out the back door. Shep took off as if he had been cooped up for days. He was running under the apple trees, through the orchard and Twing was trying to stay up with him, jumping over sprinklers and swinging onto branches. He was feeling good again. He grabbed an apple and bit into it. Sweet and crunchy. "What luck," he thought,

Masama is only a few miles from here. This is a great place to try to make contact. In fact, I'll let my hair grow, let my mustache grow, get an old hat and maybe no one will recognize me. I've got to figure out a way to make contact though, without giving myself away."

An Unreal Land

Rushdie grabbed the steering wheel of the VW with both hands, swerved with the mountainside, hugged the shoulder, stayed away from the cliff. Each turn connected him more to the road. "It was like acting," he thought, "you move in and out of the dialogue, moving with the words. In that sense he was the car and Twang was the road and they had gotten to know each other playing different roles during their last year at Eton. Rushdie couldn't help but recite a few lines in the midst of their road-rhythm rendezvous.

"Oberon, I've done thy bidding. The queen is falling for the ass. Now to watch the intrigue of this pixie dust strewn in the eyes of strangers, within a dreamscape of

31

grove and grass."

Upon which Twang responded, "We, too, have fallen under its spell and cannot tell where our story ends or begins. We, too, are left running through scenes unfamiliar to us, over ground unknown to us with the hounds baying at a distance."

Eventually they stopped their theatrical frolic and looked around. A river of silver light was meandering through a valley below them. A valley of hills and meadows with pines traveling up the sides. In the wakening light a horizon of tors and crags and high mountain peaks began to emerge.

"This is an unreal land," Twang brought himself to whisper to Rushdie. They were in a shimmering sunrise after so many nights, so many years under the moon's power. A sunrise that brought life to the mountain peaks and spread out from the east until it reached the ripples in the river, blinding them with light. "This is an unreal land," Twang repeated, hardly able to contain himself. He was literally jumping up and down in the seat of his friends VW. "We did it. We did it," he laughed. Rushdie shouted back, "No, you did it. You had the intestinal fortitude to leave, to fly, to take on . . ."

Rushdie had picked up Twang at the airport late last night and they had been driving all night. First along Puget Sound then eastward towards the Cascades. They had reached Washington Pass just as the sun cracked the horizon. They drove down talking wildly of their good fortune. Here, in this incredible land, they would see each other throughout the summer.

Twang's father had not wanted to let him go. There had been a terrible family bloodletting. His mother was in tears when he left. His father threatened to disown him. All for some unknown, hidden silent past neither his mother nor his father would confess or own up to. "What was it? Why can't I leave England?" Twang had shouted at them. "You cannot hold me here!"

"But I can cut you off from my support. If you want to take on the world, then you'll have to do it by yourself," his father had shouted back.

His mother could not bear it or hear it any longer and finally persuaded both of them to step back a little, to take some time, to . . .

"They were both of the same stubborn stock," she thought. "When they had made their mind up there was no turning back. She had learned to dance with her husband, to compliment his stature but Twang had grown to compete for his space like a sapling grown alongside the old growth, a sapling that was now competing for air and light.

It was his mother who saw him off, told him to write and to call. It was his mother who gave him the pouch that he should always keep with him and it was she who told him to hide his birthmark. She could not bring herself to say why. She also knew that his father had made the arrangements for their trusted friend to fly after him. To be a guardian from a distance.

That is how she saw him off, to realize she would never hold him in the same way again, to hope and pray for a safe journey.

Exhilarating thoughts were cursing through Twang. His chest was soaring along with the wings of a golden eagle. He became airborne, born-again, only this time to flight, to unfettered movement in the clouds, not as a newborn tied to the ground and to the soft and nurturing breast but as a man who had grown with deliberation, with age-old memories, with a destiny. That's the way he felt that morning, like the world had a place for him, somewhere, something, someone was getting ready for him. Now, it was up to him. He had prepared for this. Now he felt ready to do his part. The stars had been set in motion long ago for his lifetime.

"What did his "will" have to do with it?" he wondered, yet at the same time he felt he had willed this course of action. If it had been up to his father he would have stayed in England. What was it in this journey, what was directing him to defy his father and go to the northwest of America. As he thought about his father and his mother taking him to the airport, he remembered the pouch in his pocket. He pulled it out, opened it and took out a ring. It was inlaid with different colored gems. He put it on. It fit perfectly.

Windows to the Soul

Mariah was painting when Twing came back. He watched her load up her brush and put a wash of light gray on her paper.

"I need to let this dry," she said, "before I can put on another wash. So I'll take the time to make a list of things that need some attention. Do you do anything else besides work on cars?"

"Well, I ended up doing a whole lot of maintenance around our house because my mother was working a lot. So, I can do a few things but I haven't worked on a farm. My last job was at the Cafe Cantata in Boulder Creek. I could make you a coffee latte if you have an espresso machine." She laughed, "Well I just happen to have one. We've gone espresso nuts up here in Washington. Okay, you make us a latte while I make up

36

a list."

Before she put another wash on her paper they were going over things that had been neglected. "Number one. Can you fix a door on the shed? I think it needs the hinges tightened. Number two, follow the fence around the north side and repair what you can. You might need to put new posts in. Then there's a sprinkler pipe that's leaking in several places. I'd also like to get the grass cut down a bit in the orchard so we can pick the apple's next month."

Twing was thinking there's a lot to do on a farm. "Do you live here by yourself?" he finally asked her.

"I've had someone help me over the years and Angelina, my daughter has done a lot. She's staying on Orcas Island for the summer at my sisters. I just haven't had the money to pay anyone lately."

"But," Twing interrupted her, "is your husband or the father not here?"

"He's here and he's not here," she finally said, "he disappeared some years ago. He said he was going to hike up to Blue Lake and a do some climbing. He wanted to find a place where we could all watch the Solstice. I was pregnant and couldn't walk too far. He didn't return. The next day we went up to look for him. Sheriff O'Malley and a few other friends and I scoured that lake area. We found no trace of him. For all I know he may be living up there or somewhere else or under a rockslide. I don't know . . . I've learned to live with his disappearance and Angelina thought for a long time that her daddy had gone on a long trip and would return someday. In the last year or so she is been curious about him, who he was."

"I started my watercolors not too long after he disappeared. I think it was a way of forgetting about him at first; a way of escaping from the pain of not knowing. Every time someone walked up the front door my heart felt anticipation that it might be him. After a while my watercolors took on a kind of communication with him or at least with his disappearance. That's why I paint with broad washes of color, veils if you will. Occasionally, images rise out of the veils and I imagine him trying to communicate with me. Then I would add another veil or wash of color, which would obscure the form."

"If the soul is pure color and form is more material, more matter, then I go back and forth between them. After a few years I started to call these paintings 'windows to the soul'."

Twing felt like he had been initiated into a secret world. He looked around and for the first-time saw the many watercolors around the house. In some he could make out a recognizable image, the surrounding mountains, a river scene or an orchard, with other paintings, the colors seemed to dominate the painting and he just enjoyed their richness.

"Windows to the soul," he repeated as if in a trance, as if it was a mantra. "Windows to the soul, to the soul . . ." The minutes passed and he felt a darkness overcoming his waking world. He was looking at his face in a blue gray shining, watery surface. It was a frozen image that slightly, very slightly began to move. He turned his head and his arms reached outwards. Who was he reaching for? It looked like him but the more he reached the more obscure the image became. One veil after another moved in front of the person he wanted to reach, one color after another, from blue gray to burnt sienna. He was exhausted now and he lay prone on a mat of moss surrounded by watery depths. He could not move until a tinge of light came streaming through, a viridian green light which led him into the cold water. Rippling waves encircled him and he felt like drowning, like sinking down, down, down . . .

"Ruff!" A loud yelp rang through his ears. He jerked up to see Shep's eyes staring at him. Twing ruffled his neck and got a wet tongue on his face. What a way to wake-up. Twing looked into his eyes and remembered an old song, when I was a boy, Old Shep was a pup. Over hill and valley we'd roam. "I'll bet you were that dog," he said to him.

He could smell the coffee coming from the kitchen and hopped up. Mariah was already dressed and having breakfast. "We get started early out here," she said. Twing had some cereal and told her about his dream. "I'm not sure if I'm ready to meet this brother," he finally said.

Mariah poured him some coffee and out of her own long ago fears ventured to tell him, "Sometimes we have to get ready for changes, we have to meet what we don't necessarily want to meet. We're not always ready, except, in your case, it sounds like you might want to take some swimming lessons, at least get yourself back on your feet. A farm's a good place to start." He was lost in his thoughts and only heard "a farm's a good place to start". He nodded in agreement while she looked at him and searched his face. "Where are you really from?" she wondered, "A child in a man's body, with stubble on his face, trying to find out who you are. Such a soft face . . . Well, let's get going. You can tackle the shed door. The tools are in there."

To See a Place for the First Time

"To sleep, per chance to sleep as I sink into my seat and let the New World show itself, blow itself my way," Twang quietly intoned.

"The captain has put the seat belt sign on. Please prepare for landing"

He had to change planes in New York, New York. If only he had time to see the city. The fabled city of Oz and Gotham, Superman and super poets. He had collected old blues and folk records the last few years and Bleeker Street in Greenwich Village had come up in those folk histories. "It was a time, what a time it was" he thought, "when poets walked the streets and music was put to words, when words described the new world after the war, when questioning sounds echoed over the pavement of the cobblestones of, not only Greenwich Village, but through out the underground of practically every city in this America.

"I read about it and I've heard it," he verified. The very questioning of that great American society that developed after the war while everywhere else there were shattered illusions. "How could anyone question the heroic place of America when all around the world, the results of the wars upheavals were evident," he wondered. China had fallen or risen to a great communist revolution. India had gained independence and our great English Empire began to lose its hold on the world. Revolutions toppled dictators and kings were overthrown by fanatical fundamentalists. What had happened to those dethroned rulers? Enthroned by power and heredity and dethroned by circumstance and historic 'will'."

Twang had stayed too long having a Coney Island hot dog at the airport cafe and had to run to gate 27 way over on the other side of the airport to catch his plane to Seattle. Finally he was on his way across the continent. "It will take me about five and 1/2 hours to go across and that's going 600 mph. I sure hope my friend Rushdie is going to be at SeaTac because I'm coming in very late.

"The captain has put on the seat belt sign. Please prepare for landing. It's raining in Seattle but a very pleasant 74 degrees."

Twang got his hat and his bag and was off the plane.

"Twang, Twang!" Rushdie called to him. "Hey, Rushdie, Rushdie, I say old boy, thanks for coming. Am I glad to see you."

"Yes, yes, you know what. I've got a VW bug and we're going to go along Puget Sound and then drive east into the Cascades. We've got all night. I don't have to be home until Sunday afternoon."

"Well let's be off," said Twang.

To see a place for the first-time, especially at night, is a magical experience. Looking west Twang saw the intense dark of the Puget Sound waterways. As they rolled further north the islands lit up like the stars that might have been if this sky wasn't clouded over. They headed east toward the Cascades, listening to late-night radio, talking, singing songs they knew, on the road to tomorrow.

"I feel like an eagle, Rushdie, like I'm flying for the first-time, flying, Rushdie."

His friend could only laugh and keep his eyes on the

curvy road. With no cars coming their way and no headlights ahead, they were about as alone as they could be moving up and around and along darkened gorges, cut by rivers on one side or the other. Finally there was some lunar light coming through the outlying crags and peaks of the Cascades.

Morning finally found them sitting in Betsy's Cafe in a place called Masama. They had gone over Washington Pass and descended so steeply that they felt like they had fallen into this river valley. "I'm going to stop here for a few days," Twang told his friend. "Somehow this is far enough. I want to breathe the air, breath in this new world. I'm steeped in a different history, sunk in it. I want to get used to traveling lighter, get away from family for a while. It's like a weight has been taken off my back. I've got this light body. I want to hike around, follow a river maybe fall into a river, maybe climb a mountain. I read about the climbing history here. Bully, there were some interesting characters who put their names on these mountains. Even Masama sounds exotic.

"Let's check out the cabins next-door. I want stay here for while. At least for a month, maybe through the summer. You can come up on weekends. I'll roam around. You bring the girls from Seattle."

"And you don't think I'm a girl?" asked the woman from behind the counter. It was Betsy, looking like she'd been born in the cafe, everybody's kitchen mamma. They both smiled and thanked her for the breakfast.

"Who do I talk to about renting a cabin?" Twang asked.

"See Merryweather in No. 1. She can tell you what's available," Betsy told them, "but be careful you don't walk on her carpet. She's got the cleanest cabin west of Montana."

"Thanks."

They walked out and Twang barely said, "Merryweather in Masama. I think I'm going to like this place."

Big Ben

Well, now we have the two 18 year-olds cavorting around Masama. One coming from the privileges and isolation of wealth, the other from a laid back, almost innocent valley town, one brought up in the best schools with overwhelming tradition, the other waiting for the bell to ring so he could take a ride to the beach, one held in check by circumstance and a great family secret, the other open to the redwoods and the waves of the Pacific. Would they have anything in common besides their looks? And how are they going to meet? In order to answer those questions we've got to give others a chance to play their part in this cavorting and daydreaming and scheming. One of these is a man who has spent much of his life accumulating trivia while waiting for and making sure nothing happens to Twang.

46

"Masama comes from the Spanish, meaning 'mountain goat'. At least that's what the brochure said. I didn't realize the Spanish came this far north. Maybe it was a lone traveler. There is also a Goat Cliff and a Goat's Peak that I saw on the map. Apparently this is mountain goat country, much like the mountain country I was brought up in." Ali ben Abend mused to himself as he became acquainted with his new home while holding a hot cup of coffee between his hands. It had been years since he had traveled out of England and now, here he was, in a small town close to the border of Canada in the northwest corner of the United States.

Traveling had reminded him of his first day in London many years ago. He, and a few of his friends, loyal followers of a king who had escaped from a revolution's upheaval and taken refuge in England were walking in Piccadilly Square, enjoying, for the first time in several years, the civilized hustle and bustle of a great historic metropolis.

Unfortunately, not everyone in this city was as civilized as he and his friends would have liked. Before they could take in the surrounding pubs they were confronted with several raggedy looking kids with magenta and neon blue hair standing on end who were insistent on blocking the sidewalk in front of them. One of them, gathered up his ripped up holy black leather jacket and stuck his safety-pinned nose in the face of Ali Ben Abend and said, "Wowee, look what we've got here! A couple of rug weavers. Hey, where's your magic carpet?" Ali didn't quite know what to make of this but he wasn't going to back down. He'd been through a revolution and this strange character was not going to bother him, if he could help it.

Magenta-hair's friend now joined in on the derision until it became a wild street scene. Finally, Ali, in a calm voice simply said, in broken English, "Please, excuse us." But the street kids were just beginning and getting nastier when they heard the loud bong of Big Ben, the clock tower of history. The magenta-haired kid looked up and Ali knew that this was his chance to turn things around. He took one tiger-like lunge at the kid's belly and sent him flying into a nearby garbage can . By this time a Bobby had come by wondering what the fuss was about. The rest of the kids scattered and the garbage can moved down the street.

"Are you all right?" asked the Bobby. "Yes, thank you," Ali answered, "that boy heard the bong of the clock and I jumped at him."

"Yes, that was Big Ben," the Bobby answered, "it sounds like you were saved by the bell."

Ali's friend Tigris also thought this was an appropriate coincidence for his friend, almost like getting initiated with a new name in this new country. "Big Ben," he said out loud to his friend. "Big Ben, yes, I think it suits you."

Big Ben chuckled at the memory of that day and was astounded at how vivid it still was, however, he couldn't help thinking about how long ago it was. "Where had the years gone? He'd given up marriage and a family of his own just to remain loyal to his friend the deposed king. The king's son had become his son but with a major difference, it was always from a distance. He was always watching, looking out for Twang without Twang knowing he was under the watchful eye of a trusted guardian.

Big Ben's royal friend, the king, had taken care of him throughout the years. He had a cottage near Henley on Thames but had usually been situated in a guesthouse near Twangly's school. It had been his place to watch out for Twangly throughout these years. Only a few times had they actually seen each other but Ben was fairly sure Twangly had not recognized him as anyone other than someone passing by or sitting in a house or on a park bench.

That's how it had been for close to 18 years and fortunately there had not been any major incident or threat on Twangly's life, at least none that he knew about. Now he was reading the brochures and gathering information of the surroundings of a wandering Twangly. Ironically, he felt like a liberated Ali ben Abend.

He checked his global locator, a small video screen, moved the map around, located the Northwest and finely honed in on the Methow River Valley region. He had been following a position point or blip ever since he landed at the SeaTac airport. Now, here he was in a local espresso cafe in Winthrop, Washington. If he wanted to try some gold panning it was right next to his table. A flue had been set up by the owners for anyone to try their hand at finding gold nuggets. It looked like fun but his interest was in finding the whereabouts of another precious metal, a quartz jewel that had very unusual properties. These properties included giving off or transmitting an electrical pulse, which could be picked up on his global locator. The position point was very close to him, very close to Winthrop. He needed to detail it, bring it in . . .

"Haw's it going?" A gravelly voice startled him. "Oh, ahh, fine," he looked up to see a lean, weather-beaten old man in a large cowboy hat. "Looks like you got yourself one of those computer gadgets," he continued.

"It's a new video game," not wanting to bring any more attention to it or himself.

"Just traveling through?" The old man asked.

"Yes."

"Well, you picked a good place to stay. This is God's country, this here's the Methow River Valley."

"It is quite beautiful," Ben acknowledged. "Can you recommend any accommodations?"

"Waall, there's the Oregon Trail Motel just down the road here. An old friend of mine runs it. Just tell them Jim Bridger sent you."

"Jim Bridger, isn't that the name of an early explorer here?"

"Waall, maybe it is" he tipped his hat and sauntered out with Big Ben looking after him.

Ben paid for his coffee and drove to the Oregon Trail at the north end of town. The vacancy sign was still on and it looked like the right spot for a reconnaissance, right off Highway 20, going north to Masama and over the Cascade passes.

"Room 12," the desk clerk told him. He got his luggage and moved in. Now to monitor the position points he had established at the cafe. He turned his "video game" back on and waited for the global positioner to come into view. Again his point came on over the Masama and Winthrop area. "That's interesting," he thought as he panned and scanned the screen, "there seems to be, there seem to be two points that have gotten very close to each other. How can that be? Two points? The transmitter or the blip he had followed had gone from Seattle north over the Cascades and into the Methow Valley, very close to Masama. Now another point had blipped its way from the southern end of the Valley north to Winthrop. He decided to call his colleagues. "I'd like to make a long distance call," he told the desk clerk.

"Hello, Big Ben here, is this Tigris, hello, hello,"

"Hello, this is Euphrates. It had better be important, Ben. It's 5 a.m. here."

"I'm not sure," Ben said, "but my Global positioner is picking up two blips. They seem to be converging around Masama and Winthrop which are 14 miles apart."

"You must be picking up a duplicate transmission. Check the positioner, Ben. Reset it. If that doesn't help, you may have to send it back to Seattle. Do you know where Twangly is?"

"My last position for him was coming into Masama," Ben replied.

"See if you can find him and try to keep him in physical contact. His mother would like you to call in every two days or so. Take care, Ben. Oh, by the way, I know it's impossible but there is one other highly remote possibility for another blip."

"What's that?" asked Ben.

"The other ring."

"What do you mean? The other ring?"

"Well, when we first started using the global positioner to pick up the signal from Twangly's ring it was known that there were two old rings with similar stones and with similar properties. We know that Twangly has one and I assumed the other had been left in the Palace when we evacuated, when it was run over by the Radicals. The king never mentioned it but they had been passed down from antiquity, from as far back as the city of Urum, 4000 years ago."

"So, there is another ancient ring," thought Ben. "It never ceases to amaze me. The things I don't know. I probably never asked the right questions. Why wasn't he told about this? Maybe he had followed the wrong blip on other occasions. The range of the stones, however, was only a hundred or so miles, as far as he knew."

The family and the only ring, he assumed, had been in England all these years. His thinking was that the ring had been Twangly's because he was also in proximity to where Twangly lived. "What was the other blip? His colleagues had eluded to another ring but that was impossible," he thought, "no one had been in America that he knew about."

He had to get more information from his colleagues. This was not a malfunction. Another transmitter or ring was being picked up by his global positioner. He had watched it come up the Methow River highway and now it seemed stationary in Winthrop. As far as he knew he had picked up the other blip outside of Seattle going east over the Washington pass and ending up in Masama. That was Twangly. What or who is the other?

Free Radical Turbans

We know there are two rings because both of our 18 year-olds were given a pouch which held the precious jewels, jewels which were encased in rings in the form of a peacock and had been passed on, year after year, from one empire to another to another to another in one form or another all the way back from the great empire of Urum. The transmitting properties of these rings came from a quartz-like stone embedded in the tail of the peacock. This property had been discovered during the reign of the king when radio receivers were being developed and an odd signal kept coming from the king's ancient wealth where the rings were kept.

When the revolution occurred much of the ancient

wealth including the two precious rings had been taken out of the country by the king and his family but the Free Radical Turbans had accomplished much of what they had set out to do. They had overthrown the royal power and established their own fundamental fanatical power. The fear that the king and his many loyal followers would try to regain their power and the ancient throne caused their new leader to issue a threat and a reward. First he warned that anyone mentioning the king or his family would be beheaded and that a $100,000 reward would be paid for the death of any heir the king would have.

That was over 18 years ago and now we see the results of that fanaticism. Most, if not all, of the people of that small kingdom, had learned to live with the new political reality except for two very unusual characters. They could never quite get over the _excitement of the revolution and the possibility of carrying out the decree of their leader. For 18 years they had done every manner of make shift-work, waitering, driving taxis, shoe-shining and waited nights and days and nights for some word from their source, their spy in the king's new household in England telling them when the heir would leave England. You see, in the decree it was stated that an heir could not be killed in England because of the political consequences the new regime, the Free Radical

Turban regime might face. Finally, after 18 years of waiting, they had gotten word that Twangly had left England for a trip to the northwest United States. Here was their chance. When they arrived in Seattle they rented a white van, which they could sleep in and live in while on their quest. It was just a happen stance, a foolish thought which turned out to be right, that they ended up in the Amtrak station the very same time Twing with his guitar birthmark was standing in line for a ticket. Radical 26, who was behind him, also bought a ticket to Wenatchee while Radical 2 drove the white van across the southern pass of the Cascades. They had discussed, actually argued for hours the question of giving a warning to Twangly and in a moment of fanatical honor they decided they would follow their old tradition of giving a warning to a condemned man, primarily so that they would be vindicated for taking on the role of God when it came to taking someone's life. In one way it was like giving a last meal to a man who was to be shot at dawn. This warning would come in the form of a tape recording, which would self-destruct after it was played, at least that's what the intention was.

After leaving the tape recorder on Twing's seat with Twangly's name on the bag Radical 26 had made himself scarce, actually staying under a blanket and sleeping until the train pulled into Wenatchee. He quickly got off the train and expected to see Twangly get off also. He did not get off. At least he didn't see him. "How did he miss him? Could he still be on the train or what?" he wondered.

He waited for him on the station platform but no one else got off. He went into the parking lot and found his comrade driving up in the white van.

"Where is he?" Radical 2 asked.

"I don't know. He didn't get off the train. At least no one got off who looked like him. Maybe he took our warning seriously or maybe he reported it to the conductor."

"You did have the message erased?"

"It should have, it's worked before."

"So there is no record of it."

"As far as I know."

"Let's drive on to the next station and see if he gets off there."

They found out that the next stop for the train was Ephrata and they might have beat the train if they hadn't been stopped by the only highway patrol officer in a 500 mile radius. Fortunately, he only gave them a warning and they decided to stay within the speed limit the rest of the way. This stroke of luck, however, was not appreciated by Radical 2 and he was continually fuming at the possibility that they might have lost him.

"We're going to have to make up some more time. I don't see how you could have lost him? Were you sleeping or something? If Twangly is not at that station we're going to have to drive up to that Masama or whatever place he was asking about. I don't think you have any idea what's at stake here. We cannot allow Twangly to get back to England. We've got to take care of him, and then we will finally rid ourselves of the last vestige of the old order. It will be gone, a thing of the past."

"Okay, okay," Radical 26 cut in, "Don't go off again, we've been waiting for this for a long time. Twangly has finally left England. We know he's around here. We've seen him, we've warned him and it's time we finally get a chance at the money."

Radical 2 snorted back, "I just hope we're still going to get paid for this. The price put on his head was years ago and the condition was that it not happen in England. Now we have our chance or . . .maybe we've lost it"

"Look, it's been 18 years. Can Twangly still be a threat?"

"Don't talk like that. The revolution requires that we carry out our leaders decree."

"Even after all these years?"

"What have we lived for then?" We spent our lives

waiting for this."

"That is immaterial at this point. We don't have him. We may have lost him. We heard him ask questions about Masama. We can assume that's where he's heading. Look! We're coming on to the next station."

"Do you see anyone?"

"I don't see anything. Drive around."

They only saw a single car leaving the parking area and driving away.

"Nothing, no one, the train may not have come yet or it may have left already."

They waited in the dark of a mid-Washington night. Waiting, again, as they had for 18 years since the revolution had brought them together, since their revolutionary fervor had caused the King to fall. "The King's heresy," they intoned, "had brought it on himself and their revolution had triumphed." For 18 years they had carried on personal vows that they would carry out the final decree, which was to rid themselves of the King's heir. But 18 years had taken its toll on their fervor and now they questioned and debated their undertaking. Their lives, however, had been fed by the revolution and they had not filled them with any other cause or reason. They were the old guard, the Free Radical Turbans, the true revolutionaries. After 18 years they had seen the results of their upheaval. Their great leader had passed on and the revolution had continued. There was no turning back. The King and his Queen had found sanctuary in

England. They had taken on new names. Their son had become Twangly Rexroth and he had gone to English schools. They had lived quietly on a guarded estate near Henley on Thames and they had kept this incredible secret and turbulent past away from their son and their neighbors.

"We let him slip away," an exasperated Radical 2 groaned.

"At this point we should not attract attention to ourselves," retorted Radical 26, Let's go back to Wenatchee and go north from there. Remember, he asked the clerk about Masama. We heard him say that. It's a small dot on our map. It's just north of Winthrop."

"Let's go find him and finally get what's coming to us."

The Secret of the Queen

Dr. Highshe and his companion Camec had lived with the secret of the king and queen and their lives as the Rexroths for 18 years. Dr. Highshe had been loyal to his friend the King. They had both been born in the year of the comet Tahoe Tech. They played together in the gardens of the Palace. They grew up with possibilities and expectations. They found a bond between them that would not be broken even when the world turned upside down and Dr. Highshe was forced to choose between his friend, the king and leadership in the revolution. No, he stayed loyal to his friend. When they left their homes, their hopes for a modern country had been destroyed by the Free Radical Turbans.

Both had gone to Cambridge University. His close friend, the future King, was called back to their country to take on the crown, to sit on the peacock throne. His father, the monarch, had died and left the country in mourning. Thus his close friend, his colleague, was called to travel a path ordained by his birth. He would become the next ruler of the peacock throne. He, however, had his studies and proceeded to put his mind and will into them. He would become a doctor and it would be several years before they would see each other again. Only their correspondence kept their friendship alive.

Dear High,

I find it amazing. Everyone looks up to me. Whatever I want is available to me. I don't have to work for good grades.

I feel a responsibility to carry out my father's desires, to change our country, to bring it into the 20th century. I'm not sure where to begin?

I'm hoping you can join us when you're done with your studies. Dr. Highshe sounds important.

Yours,

Peacock Bill.

Dear Ruler of the Peacock,

I received your letter and can only tell you that the internship is grueling. It's like the final push to weed out those who can not master 12 to 14 hour days of study, testing and patient analysis; those who find it too stressful and those who can muster it. One of our colleagues was found in the Thames the other day. They say it was an accident but I'm not sure.

I will make it and look forward to seeing you and talking about your hopes of change. With sincerity,

Dr. Tobe

For several years letters continued until the summer before Abe Highshe's graduation. He was invited to the Kings wedding and packed his bags to go. What a time it was. For three days there was celebration in the country. For three days they toasted and dreamed of a grand beginning. Then he went back to Cambridge to finish his degree. After some months he received another letter from the king.

Dear old friend Doctor to be,

Ruling the country is probably like an unending internship only the hours are longer. I've never seen such entrenched thinking, particularly among the religious leaders. We have wonderful traditions here but they are constantly being narrowed down by the dogmas of exclusion. I'm convinced our future lies in expanding our role in the world and that means moving towards more representation by our people. It also means more personal rights and there you have the major problem. A few powerful religious leaders are adamant about keeping their control or power over the people. They cite the holy books but I believe it's their power they want to exercise and continue.

We need people like you my friend. Come back and we will find a place for you.

Yours,
the Peacock throne

Their hopes were high but neither one of them realized just how strong the attraction was for the fundamentalists in their society. Everything that was wrong was because the people were not following the laws of the holy books and everything that kept the people secure in their positions was because the people were fulfilling all of the laws. Change is not easy for any individual let alone a whole society.

Doctor Highshe was put in charge of education and there the opposition began to mount. The religious leaders would not allow any education that was not proscribed by the their holy books.

It was a valiant effort by the young ruler and a few of the idealistic, hopeful followers he had put into government positions. It was also the beginning of chaos. Violence had erupted in the countryside. The King was forced to send in his army to restore order and keep reforms intact, particularly in the schools. In the ensuing confrontation a few prisoners of fundamentalist beliefs were taken. Without the King knowing it and through his appointed commanders these prisoners were subjected to inhuman treatment by their guards. When this news was spread around the villages, and the faithful followers, a grand swell of fear and fanaticism began in the country.

It was in this political arena that the Queen gave birth to the next heir. All the papers were headlined with the great news but it was Dr. Highshe's diary that revealed the truth of the events.

November 2nd,
The Queen's situation was critical when I

was called. Her hand nurse Camec had labored with her until she felt it was time. When I examined her I heard two heartbeats and told her to get ready for twins. The Queen was already hysterical from the contractions.

When the first child came there was no sound. He was blue and I cut the umbilical cord wrapped around his neck. I told the nurse to take him into emergency care, while I helped the Queen with the second. It was another boy in fine condition and howling as soon as his head gained the freedom to breathe.

This child was put to the breast of the Queen and she declared, "this will be the next heir to the throne."

When the King heard of the birth of his son he was ecstatic. The Queen made Camec and I vow never to mention the other child. The King and all the world only know of one child born today. Thus I was put in charge of the first-born. No one acknowledged the tradition of the first born, but it was this tradition that required the next heir to be the first-born male child.

November third,

It was an old wife's tale or a soothsayer's rantings but the nurse could barely relay what had been said about the new heir.

"A soothsayer had said a child would be born who would unrightfully be designated the heir to the throne. In this deceit an ancient curse would be carried out. The power of the ruler would end and the peacock throne would crumble. The true line of the ruler would grow up in a foreign land, his parents would know terror and finally freedom without power. When the true line of the ruler is reconciled with the deceitful line a new era would emerge."

November 5th,

I was not able to write yesterday. I was making arrangements to have the other child taken out of the country. His progress was remarkable and I could condone his disappearance. The paperwork was taken care of and the child was to be adopted by an American family. The father works for an oil exploration branch of the Kings oil concern. He is to take the child back to California where we have an office in America.

By the time this is taken care of no one will know of a second child, not even the King. His secret will be the Queen's, who thinks he died, the nurse and myself and we have sworn secrecy to the Queen to not talk of this other child to anyone. If they were to even see each other they have identical birthmarks on their necks. These will be their markings in the world.

November 6th,

Today we sent off the rightful heir of the King. I made one concession that I hope will not indict me. Out of the royal jewels which the King has entrusted me I gave one of the Rings of Urum to the father of the child. It was in a wrapped pouch. I told him this is for the child and is to be given to him when he is 18 years old. It is his one connection to his past.

There is one other ring from the same time. Both are made from the same stone, a very rare quartz with unusual properties.

This other ring will be kept for the son of the King growing up in his household.

November 9,

The times are tumultuous. I must lock the diary away or the truth will come out.

Mariah

From those perilous days of the revolution, through all these years of growing, changing and waiting it may be time to review where the current chain of events has brought the twin brothers and our cast of characters. Doctor Highshe and Camec took their first vacation in many years and it just so happened it was shortly before Twangly left for Seattle to meet his friend Rushdie. They traveled up the California coast and ended up giving Twing an anonymous letter, which told him that he had a twin brother. They also told him that this brother might be up in the vicinity of Masama in the state of Washington, which started Twing on his journey north. Big Ben, the faithful guardian of Twangly had followed him to Masama but had lost him except for an electronic blip on a global locater screen. He also seemed to be spending more time at Betsy's Cafe than he was looking for Twangly. The two Radicals had heard that Twangly had left England and thought this was their chance to do him in but they inadvertently saw Twangly's twin brother Twing at the train station and ended up following him only to lose him in Wenatchee. After a nasty incident when he lost his backpack Twing was picked up by Jim Bridger and ended up on a farm owned by Mariah West who painted strange watercolor pictures. Let's get back to Twing and see how he is doing on the farm.

"You do have an unusual birthmark," Mariah said, as she looked at Twing's neck. "It reminds me of an electric guitar. Your girlfriends must have liked playing it." He just stammered and told her about the letter he had received and how two people had left it in the Cafe Cantata where he was working. Mariah was very interested and very excited to think that she might be part of this mystery. She wanted to hear the tape also. He put the earphones on her and all she heard was a flute and a sitar with a drum accompaniment.

"Are you sure you heard something else?" she asked him.

"Yes, there was something else, a warning that I swear I heard but it obviously is not in there now, so maybe I imagined it. I don't know at this point. All I know is that I didn't get off at Wenatchee and I ended up here."

"My mother told me I was adopted when I told her about his letter. It was a real shocker. I mean you grow up in a world that you think you know, that was your home, your family, your friends, even a past that I could claim as my own. Now I find out I've got a different past. I don't know if that frees me or ties me to something else. At least it's awakened a longing in me to find out about my real past and a brother . . . I may have brother, a twin brother. Can you imagine that? He's supposed to be around Masama. How am I going to make contact?"

"Okay, let's take that warning seriously for a minute," Mariah interjected. "Suppose I put a note on the bulletin board of the Masama general store. What would make this brother call you?"

"I don't know," Twing answered.

"All right, let's take another approach. What if I drove up there and just looked around for while. Or maybe I could just ask Betsy, who runs the cafe, to look for me. Does he look like you?"

"Well, the note said that it was a twin brother. Maybe he does. You'll notice, though, I've been trying to change my looks so I won't be recognized by . . ."

"I hadn't noticed," Mariah laughed, "You mean

those hairs on your chin?"

"Oh, come on now, that's a goatee and in the finest tradition. What about my ponytail? Don't I look a lot different than a week ago?"

Twing grabbed an old cowboy hat, put on some dark glasses, a denim jacket and proceeded to stroll across the living room floor.

"Mama, don't let your sons grow up to be cowboys," he drawled.

Mariah just laughed and said, "All right, all right, you've convinced me. They'll never recognize you but I think I had better drive to Masama. In fact I'll call on old Jim Bridger and we'll go up together to see if we can find someone who looks like you."

"But, let's think of a note we could put up. Something that would give your brother a hint or at least so he might come into the cafe at a certain time."

"But what?"

"Well, we could say, 'Lost brother. Has birthmark in shape of guitar on neck. Meet you in Betsy's cafe on Saturday 10 a.m. Found brother'."

"I don't know if we should say 'brother' or even mention the birthmark?" Twing responded.

"But that's the only distinguishing mark you have."

"Ooh, that hurts."

"But it still might be too risky. Let me go there and

ask Betsy first. It he's there, he'll probably stop in at the cafe. If that doesn't work let's put up a note."

"Okay, we're back to what to write."

"Lord, who ever left that warning on the tape, whoever did, must be pretty sophisticated or were they? I mean why would they have left a warning anyway? Were you going to go back home and dump this?"

"Let's take a chance."

"How about, 'Lost brother. Guitar birthmark on neck. Meet me in Betsy's cafe on Saturday 10 am', or 'Lost friend. Guitar birthmark on neck. Meet me in Betsy's cafe on Saturday 10 am'."

"We'll have to take a chance on the birthmark. It's the only thing that might connect us. The letter mentions that we both have one."

"How do they know?"

"They?"

"Yes, the couple who left you the letter in Boulder Creek?"

"I don't know."

"Okay, I'll do it." Mariah said, "I'll drive up tomorrow morning and spend some time at Betsys."

"Now, I've got to show you something." She took Twing to her studio and showed him her latest watercolor. A misty blue green atmospheric picture with distinct dark gray forms in the middle. He moved back from it.

"It looks like you're in the form phase or at least it looks like forms are pushing out," he ventured to say, trying to sound like he had mastered the vocabulary.

"It's strange, but the more color washes I put on, the stronger those forms become. I'm not sure what to make of it. Step back some more. Look at it. It's almost like a building, the ruins of a building."

"It does have the outline of an old house. So, it's time to destroy it. Give it a sienna wash, a strong one."

"All right, that's for this afternoon. I also want to call Jim, to see if he would come with me tomorrow. He's like an old scout. He'll sniff out your brother if there is one."

"I don't know how much I want anyone else to know about this."

"Oh, Jim is the most trusted man I know. It's like he's part of the whole community here. If you want anyone to help you it would be Jim."

"Well, I'm going to finish off the last of the fence posts this afternoon."

"'Mending fences', wasn't that a poem by Robert Frost?"

"Yes, yes, I think so but I've forgotten the words."

Twing grabbed the old cowboy hat and headed for the door. "Mama, don't let your sons grow up . . ."

faded away as he walked to the eastern edge of the farm.

In the afternoon, Mariah sat down and laid another wash over her painting. It was a strong sienna color, almost opaque. It should have covered much of the subtlety of the atmosphere, of the blue green. Instead it brought out darker blue gray forms, forms that took on more distinction as she allowed it to dry, forms that further defined an old broken down building. "What was coming through here?" She wondered. "It's been years since I've felt something coming into my paintings." She felt the memory of someone, someone who she thought had finally died . . .

"What are you trying to do?" She burst out. "This is crazy. It's a piece of paper with some colors on it. It has no more connection to anything else except in my mind. Except in my mind?" she repeated as if to convince herself.

No matter how hard she wanted to deny it she sensed that something was going on. At the least it was agitating her. Each time she looked at her painting the forms became more distinct. Now she started to see an old broken down cabin near a lake. Had she painted that? Where did that come from? Was it just something she was interpreting, seeing in the painting?

She left the room, not asking any more questions. She knew enough to be patient, to let time play a part. She had watched her paintings change years ago. Slowly she had settled into a style with them. She thought her paintings had coincided with the acceptance of her husband's disappearance and also with the growth of her daughter, who had filled up more and more of her life. Today, it seemed like something new or something else was coming into her paintings.

She called Jim and told him about Twing and his hopes of finding his brother.

"I also want you to look at my current painting," she told him, "can you come tomorrow?"

Jim drawled on about seeing Betsy. "She owes me some biscuits and gravy. I brought some firewood up to her place last week. I'll pick you up in the morning around nine."

"Evermore"

Twing had seen it on his way to the field. On his way to fixing the fence posts he had noticed a wheel pushing out of a tarp covered with old tires, under hay and other debris. He uncovered some more of the wheel. The tire was flat and it was on the rusty green body of an old army jeep. "Wow, a relic, an old war relic!" he shouted to the raven sitting a few feet away. He moved debris until he could pull the top of the tarp off. There, in all its past glories stood the rusted remains of a World War II army jeep. To anyone else it would have been buried or sold for scrap. To Twing it was an old beauty. "I can restore this," he said to the raven. "You'll see it shine once again, move again, fly again." "Squack, squack," he heard from the raven. "He laughed and answered back, "I'll call it 'Evermore'."

That was the day after he had arrived. He talked to
Mariah about it that night. She did not want to hear
about it but he insisted. She confided that it was her late
husband's. They had found it parked by the Methow
river after he disappeared. She had brought it home
waiting for him, waiting, hoping he would come. She did
not want to be reminded. It is gone for me just like he is.

"Take it, bury it. Do whatever you want with it but
don't mention to me again."

Twing wasn't sure what to think. He was elated with
his find, yet felt her pain with the past. He was
determined to try and rectify it. No, he wanted to restore
this relic and he hoped it would bring something positive
into her life, something or some way that may help heal
a wound that was still painful.

That is how Twing spent the first week. He helped
Maria with the most pressing of the left over
maintenance projects, even helped her feed a few
chickens and the two horses in the morning. In the late
afternoon and on into the night he worked on Evermore.
He took apart one piece of machinery after another,
took apart the generator, the carburetor, the radiator,
checked the valves. The engine was still in good shape.
He was in his element. Ever since his father died he had
been working on cars, from toy cars to push cars to his
mother's car and finally the neighbor's cars. He loved

the smell of oil, the feel of smooth milled steel, the perfect surfaces, the purr of a well-tuned engine. He remembered the hours he had spent under the hoods and bodies of cars. Those days were filled with the music of his favorite radio station. He lived with the top 10 songs while he changed the spark plugs. His young emotional life was punctuated with the pop music of the last 30 years. Squacked the raven, "evermore."

"Mariah, I need to go into Winthrop. I need some things." He didn't want to tell her everything "I need to get a hinge for the shed and some more wire clips for those fence posts."

"Take the pickup this afternoon and buy yourself some new jeans while you're at it." She handed him a $20 dollar bill. "That's for all the work you've been doing. You can charge the hinge and nails at the Bate and Tackle hardware store. It's on the Main Street. Just don't hang around too long. You've been warned, you know." She joked with him but there was a hint of seriousness in her voice. "Jim Bridger and I are going to Masama in the morning. We're going to do some scouting for your long-lost brother."

He put his hair in a ponytail, took his old cowboy hat and pulled the collar of his jacket over his neck.

"I thank I'm ready" he drawled.

He hopped in her old Ford pickup and felt like the

wind was carrying him. He let the gravel fly. Geez, it felt good. He turned on the local radio station and played with the dial until "the Boss" was singing about being born in the USA.

He was oblivious to the white van parked along the lake road just outside of Winthrop. He drove right past the Oregon Trail motel. He was singing along with the boss. He was thinking about the gasket he needed and the spark plugs and the air filter. "That baby is going to purr when I'm through with her."

He gave little thought to the taped warning he had gotten on the train. It seemed like a long time ago. Its effect had waned, particularly here in the openness of the fields and the orchards he walked through. It was a land open to the sky. He had not forgotten his real quest, however, and that was underneath everything he did. Even his excitement at rebuilding the old jeep had his brother in mind. Maybe he could buy it from Mariah and when or if he finds his brother they could ride around the country. He had no idea who this person was but he felt he had to find him. This was his quest. This he could sing. And he sang for the whole world to hear,

> "This is my quest.
> No matter how hopeless,
> No matter how long."

This was his impossible dream.

Dreams

And what were the dreams of Radical 2 and Radical 26. They sat in their white van biding their time as they had for 18 years. At least here they could go swimming in Pearrygin Lake between their trips to Winthrop and Masama. They had taken in the mini golf course in Winthrop where both of them had become objects of enjoyment by the locals. Radical 2's golf ball was consistently short and Radical 26's ball was consistently outside of their lane. If there was an immediate dream of Radical 26 it may have been to beat his comrade in arms at this golf game so that he could get his double scoop ice cream cone paid for by his comrade. As it was they had also become occasional customers of the

Masama general store and Betsy's cafe next to it. They had temporarily lost Twang but were determined to exhaust the area until they could get the next clue. They were more observers than questioners, besides they had accents, which would make them too obvious to the locals. It was Twing who unknowingly saw their white van parked in the state camping lot next to the lake road. He was on his way to Winthrop. They were sitting outside of their van playing backgammon. Their lives crossed but they may as well have been a continent away.

What dreams did Big Ben have as Twing drove past the Oregon Trail motel. Big Ben, was biding his time between Winthrop's gold-panning coffee house and driving north to Masama to Betsy's Cafe. Betsy had become interested in his "video game" and he enjoyed the attention from this kitchen mama. He was staying in touch with his colleagues at the estate but he had very little news for Twangly's mother. He still had the two blip problem. One blip had stopped over Masama and one had stayed over Winthrop. At least it looked like that. They hadn't moved in days. He kept thinking they might converge into one.

As Twing returned from Winthrop he felt tempted to drive the few miles north to Masama. He wanted to realize this dream of a twin brother but was also afraid of the possibility that it was all a hoax, a wild idea brought about by mistaken identities or circumstances. He was drawn to drive straight but he just did not feel ready yet and at the last moment turned right instead and went back to the farm. He had work to do and he was determined to get Evermore running again.

Omens of Gray

Jim Bridger came early the next morning. He was usually up with the sun and he looked like he hadn't slept in days, maybe years. It was the face of a thousand restless travelers. His eyes held a deep sadness, yet a spark enervated them and Mariah could not help but feel this life enter her home, her studio. She brought him right into the studio to look at her latest creation.

"Before coffee, my eyes don't focus," he slowly said.

"OK, OK, I'll bring the coffee. Just sit here and let this painting take on some life. Who knows it might look better out of focus. I can't seem to change it. No matter how many washes I put on these forms, this main image comes back."

He put his gnarled old hands around the warm cup and just breathed it in. Steam curled around him and slowly but he let the images in front of him take on definition. He was not sure he was seeing right.

"You painted this? Here? It's my granddaddy's cabin. He built it years ago. What you see there is what's left of it."

"Come on," she said incredulously, "You're imagining things. These forms, the images just kept popping out. Every time I put a light grey wash on the image it became more defined."

"It's the remains of my cabin, I tell ya, I can take you there. It's near Blue Lake, fairly well hidden. I don't know anyone else who knows about it. From 50 yards away it just blends with the rocks and fallen trees. There was a rockslide there a few years ago. This is what it looked like the last time I saw it."

Mariah sat there in silence. "How many years ago was that rock slide?" She asked him after a long moment.

"Oh, a few. It's an unstable area. That peak above Blue Lake has a history of rock slides."

"Was it about 10 years ago?" she asked.

"I recall it was."

Mariah felt her body become limp. A wave of emotion swept over her. She could not stand.

"Jim, Jim"

He held her, with the strength of an old standing trunk, he held her.

"What is it? Mariah"

"Jim, its, it's Comet, he's coming through. He's showing me. After so many years he's telling me something, and you, you're the interpreter, you needed to see this, Jim. He's telling us something. I want to go there. When can we go there?.

"Whoa, slow down, Nellie. Sit down. Let's take one thing at a time. First, we're going to Masama. We've got something to take care of, remember. We can talk about it on the way to Betsy's."

She was still in an excited state when she waved to Twing who was working in the shed.

"Bye, Twing, we'll see you tonight."

She got into Jim's pickup and they left the farm.

Betsy's Cafe

It was a quick 14 miles to Betsy's, punctuated with Mariah's question, "what is he trying to tell me, Jim?"

"Let's solve one mystery at a time, shall we. Today we are going to see if there's anything at all to your young friend's story. I mean, what do we have to go on? He tells you that he received a note from two people who stopped in to see him or saw him at the cafe he worked at in Boulder Creek, California. They told him that he has a twin brother who he was separated from at birth and that this twin brother was now up in the vicinity of Masama. On the way he finds a tape recorder on his seat in the train that warns him about carrying out or pursuing his trip to Masama. Then the warning disappears. I mean, there's no evidence of the warning."

"He does have the letter about his twin brother, though," interjected Mariah.

"All right, maybe it was a set up from the start," answered Jim.

"But his mother admits that he was adopted," continued Mariah.

They fell into silence and realized they had come to Masama. "If there was anyone here who looked like Twing it should not be too hard to find out," asserted Mariah. "After all," she continued, "Masama has a general store, Betsy's Cafe and a few cabins that are rented out and we have a note we can post on the bulletin board if nothing happens today."

There were other vacation homes or cabins around but this was the hub of Masama and anyone visiting here would most likely stop in here at some time. They just had to ask the right questions.

"Well, lookee here, it's the Westwind and the Old Scout. I ain't seen you in the month of Sundays."

"Moooorning, Betsy," Jim made morning sound slower than usual. I need some of your rot gut coffee"

"Hey now, we're going upscale here, you know it's fresh roasted right out of Seattle."

"You mean it's got to smell a lot but it won't have a bite to it. Let's put it this way, if my spoon won't stand in it, it can't be your coffee."

She shrugged him off and looked at Mariah, "I ain't seen you in a long time. What's new on the farm?"

"Well, we've got several things to talk about and we're gonna order some breakfast this morning. You still have that good sausage gravy and biscuits?"

"I can make you some, but what's up."

"We're hanging out today. Actually, we're doing some investigating work."

"Oh yeah, what are you investigating?"

Mariah lowered her voice as if she was playing detective. She looked around the cafe. There were only two other people in the cafe, two older men sitting in a booth reading the local paper. Nothing unusual except that they both wore similar camouflage pants. She couldn't get a good look at their faces.

"Betsy, we're looking for a young man, 18, about 160 pounds, sort of a lean face with a birth mark on his neck." She leaned even closer, "in the shape of a guitar."

The newspapers rustled.

Betsy didn't know if Mariah was serious or not. She got them coffee and before she went over to the other two customers, told them about a young man who had been in several times but not in the last few days. "Wait a minute, wait a minute, he asked me about a good backpacking trail. I told him to check with the store. I think he may have gone backpacking somewhere. But, if this is the guy, I believe he was staying in one of the cabins, because he signed his bill with some strange name, Twist or something. I think I called him Twitty, like Conway Twitty, the country singer"

The newspapers rustled again.

Mariah turned around. "Maybe I should put on a song."

"Play S3 for me," Betsy blurted out as Mariah headed for the jukebox.

"Do you remember which cabin he charged it to?" asked Jim, not wanting to waste any time.

The classic juke box whirled with colors and started playing, "Somebodies needin' somebody, the way I do . . ."

Betsy thought for a second and said, "I think, I think, if I remember right, wait a minute . . ."

She took some more hot water to the camouflaged men. They were ready to pay the bill. She gave them change.

"A half cup more," one of them said, "and thanks".

"That's on oldie, gentlemen," she said to them as she joined in on the words, "Somebodies wantin somebody, they can hold on too . . . That's my boy, Conway,

Conway Twitty. Thanks gentlemen. See you tomorrow."

She joined Mariah at the jukebox and they both walked back to the counter. "Where was I, oh, yeah, yeah. He was staying in either seven or eleven. You could check with Pager in the office or Merryweather. What's all this about anyway?"

"Were not sure yet, but if there's some truth to it we're helping to find an old relative."

Betsy brought them their breakfast. A family with four young boys and one girl came in. One of the boys looked at Jim and whispered to another, "He's a real cowboy." The two men left. Finally, they too, were ready to leave.

"Betsy, these are still the best biscuits and gravy this side of the Cascades," Jim drawled in his raspy voice.

"Thanks, Jim"

"Will you do me a favor, Betsy?" asked Mariah, "will you call me or Jim if this Twist kid comes back in. We'd like to help somebody out if we can."

They walked over to the office and asked Pager about this "Twist" kid. Pager had joined the little community in Masama a few years ago. He had fallen in love with the country, its skiing and kayaking and biking and you name it and decided to open up a tourist office for those traveling into the Cascades. In between time he was the clerk at the Mazama general store and in the office to help Merryweather, his wife, rent out the cabins.

"Hey, Jim, Mariah, how are you doing?"

"Hello Pager, listen, we've got a favor to ask? Do you have a young guy by the name of "Twist" staying here?"

"Twist, Twist, you mean like a "twist of fate?""

"Something like that. Betsy says he might be in seven or eleven."

"Not Twist, but there is someone named Twang or Twangly in number 7."

"Wait a minute, Mariah shook her head, there's a Twang. Are you serious?"

At this Pager turned his head to see if anyone else was listening, "well, the name he's under is actually Twangly Rexroth but I couldn't let this out to anyone else but you Mariah. I owe you a few."

"Has anyone else asked about this kid?"

"Yes, actually, they were two guys in camouflage outfits not too long ago. I just told them I couldn't give out that information. I mean some people come here to get away. But that's not all. There was another guy, smaller, older with an Indian accent, I mean Eastern, more Indian Indian. Then there was his friend Rushdie, who came with him originally. He's been trying to get hold of him. He left a message to have Twangly call him, something about salmon fishing. He's a popular guy. The only thing is, he's gone backpacking. I don't know when he'll be back. He paid for the cabin for the summer."

Jim looked at Mariah. Mariah looked at him. Mariah just shook her head as she walked away and asked, "Jim, you think we're just seeing the tip of the iceberg?" I mean, are we hearing right. In one morning we've uncovered a whole potential family, along with acquaintances of all kinds including camouflaged ones. I mean, is this for real. Twingly Birdwell has a brother, a twin brother named Twangly Rexroth and they didn't know about each other and don't.

"Or will they?" interjected Jim. "Let's find out where he's gone backpacking. He may have registered at the general store or at least he should have if he's going out by himself."

"Thanks Pager, come by for some apple cider when you get a chance," Mariah reminded him as they left the office.

They looked over the register at the general store. This was the Forest Service's local registration or registrar for backpacking into the eastern side of the Cascades. They started following the names down each page. They came to a circled T. Rex, June 27, Blue Lake. The name of the campground or trail was left blank but there was only one major trail up to Blue Lake.

"T. Rex, Twangly Rex, Rex, Rexroth?"

"That might be him" Mariah said, "but let's keep checking a few more names." They went back two weeks on the register and nothing even came close to T. Rex.

"Why was it circled?"

"Maybe his friends have been here."

"Or maybe his not so friends?"

"Jim, I think we've got enough for Twing to go on but you know what is. . . .

"I'm thinking the same thing. The ruins of my great granddaddies cabin are near Blue Lake. It's the image that keeps coming up in your paintings."

"It's got to be a coincidence," Mariah answered him, shaking her head and trying to convince yourself. Years ago she would not have said something like that. Years ago she would have seen correlations in everything. They were all there for a reason. She was convinced of it. She was known as the Westwind blowing in cosmic unity. That was how she met her husband, her soul mate during those halcyon days. "It was meant to be," she had told him and he, he was the comet streaking through her time. She believed it but could not let go of him when he disappeared. He was a comet. It was a child's game and the years turned her against this ephemeral world. Even when her paintings took on images of other worlds she began to deny them and him. She buried him over and over again until all she had left was the soil and her daughter to take care of.

"This is all I coincidence," she barely said to Jim.

"Mariah, let's talk to Twing. We're on the bronco now. We've got to ride it out. Sometimes we can tame the beast, sometimes we get thrown but we've got to hang on for the ride." She just smiled and said, "you've always been there, Jim, you're like the land itself. What would I do without you?"

"You've done all right, Mariah. We've got to take the reins. We're going to get Twing and we're going to find his long lost brother."

Angelina

"I got something purring today. I mean, she started up and I felt like taking her to the dunes. What a sweet sound. She needs some cleaning up but I think we can go for a ride." Twing was doing at least 100 words per minute when they drove up. Mariah hadn't seen him like this. Jim called out "whoa boy, slowdown, what's purring?"

"The old jeep, it's cool, it's running, it's . . ."

Mariah turned from him, "I said you could take it but I didn't want to hear about it, Twing"

He caught himself and stuttered, "I, I got carried away. I'm sorry, I'll shut her off."

"I'd like to take a look at the old cat," Jim said, "that

is, if you're all right with that?" looking at Mariah.

"I'm going in," she responded, "let's talk over dinner."

Jim followed Twing to the shed. There in all its old glory was the jeep Jim had seen years ago. Even the comet was still visible on the door.

"This was Comet's. He rode around like there was no tomorrow in that thing. I got to know him. I got to know both of them. I met them when they were stranded up on Washington Pass one year. I was coming back from the Cascade Farms and saw this jeep off the highway and two wild kids in it. They were wearing their tie dies and their scarfs. They were into colors then. I gave them gas and it was all "groovy" and "wow" and "we want to return the favor"."

"Did they?" Twing asked.

"Yeah, I think they did," Jim kind of pondered. "I'm the godfather of their daughter Angelina and when Comet died or disappeared or burned-out she became like the daughter I never had. Course I didn't see her too often but I've been part of her life all these years and she's made mine."

"What's she like?"

"Well, she's kinda like a moon spirit, at least that's what I called her after that time I took her out of the house one evening. The field seemed to be covered with a strange light. We both looked up and there was the biggest full moon I had ever seen. She just glowed with it. Everything just glowed with it . . . anyway, after that I called her Angelina my little moon spirit. She did not want to go back in that night and we may have stayed out all night. I don't remember. She's the moon spirit all right."

"Where is she now?"

"Well, I think she's with Mariah's sister on Orcas Island. She's got a job for the summer at some restaurant, I think, Helga's Whole Foods Buffet. She'll probably be coming back for the 4th." He padded the warm hood. "Twing, you got yourself some history here."

"Well, I, ah, I wanted to fix it up for Mariah. I guess this is not the way to do it."

"I think she'll get over it. This thing brings back some old memories, unresolved memories. But we've got a few things to tell you also, maybe resolve, also."

They headed back into the house. Mariah and Jim told Twing of the encounters during the day. He was energized with their story.

"There's a guy named Twangly staying there?" he responded with wide eyes. "That's a little much. I mean, you think I've got a brother named Twangly. Come on, Twangly Rexroth? Who the heck is that? Where did he come from? Look, someone is putting us on, all of us."

At this point, Jim could only repeat what he said to Mariah.

"Look, Twing, we are all on the bucking bronco now and were not getting off until we either tame it or it throws us. I suggest we take a hike up to Blue Lake. There is one main trail and we would most likely pass anyone coming back down. While we are out there we could check out the remains of an old cabin we've been thinking about."

"I think we should go soon," Mariah advised, "I want to be here when . . ."

The phone rang,

"Hello."

"Hello oo, this is Pager. Is this Mariah?"

"Yes."

"Well, I'm not sure if this is important to you or Jim but the two guys who asked about Twangly . . .

"Yes!"

"The two guys in camouflage pants. The tall guy and a fat guy."

"Yes!"

"Well, they've rented cabin No. 6."

"Has Twangly come back?"

"I haven't seen him. I'm not sure if he's here or not."

"Okay, well, thanks. This may help us decide what to

do. We'll probably stop by tomorrow."

"Okay, good bye."

"See you," Mariah put down the phone and walked back to the kitchen.

"I think our agenda has filled up for tomorrow. The camouflage guys have just taken a cabin at Pager's."

"So what does that mean?" Asked Twing.

"Probably, probably . . ." Twing could barely hear Mariah's voice. It wafted like a breeze through the screen window, like a breeze in the dark moonless night as he drifted off to sleep, waves laughing at the small boat carrying them up and down. Dim objects appeared ahead of them, darker ones on all sides, like islands through which a wind could blow. Not islands of sand or soil or lava but islands of metal parts and posts and scraps of iron left over, discarded growing forms becoming larger as they rowed. Is there no sanctuary in this laughing, waving sea? Row into there, a harbor, a small round inlet, just big enough for our craft. Climb out, climb out, climb on to these cages, hang on. But the metal itself began to crumble under the weight of all of them, cheap metal, bending under them while they slowly sank into the dark sea, only the . . .

"Twing, up and at em. Coffees on. We're heading up to Masama." "Geez, thought Twing, "what a dream." He dressed with the images of the sea around him. "I need to see the morning light, man," he thought, as he stepped out the back door. There, towards the east, the horizon had dissipated, disappeared, broken down the fields around him, the expansive land was bathed in light. He rubbed his eyes. "It was as if, as if, he was bringing light, an ancient light to this part of the world."

Blue Lake

Not too far from his front entrance, a field was washed in greens and browns, the land swept up in sharp contrast, in rocky hard contrast where deep shadows still broke up the mountainside. Here, in one of these pockets of contrast lay Twang, still asleep, waiting for the light to stream through his tent just as he had done every morning for the last few days. He had picked this spot on the east side of the lake because the morning light streamed through him like a wake-up call and proceeded to turn the Blue Lake gold. That's when he got up. That's when he sat in front of his tent and just watched the rocky tors and spires surround him. Blue Lake was still being fed by the winter snow around the northern perimeter. This is not like anything he had ever experienced in Henley or England where he grew up. From his base camp he had taken hikes everyday and found places to read or write or sketch a remembrance of his exploration. Today, on this, the seventh day, he was ready to take a dip in the lake, find himself a vantage point for his last sketch and then rest for a while, before packing up to go back to his cabin at Masama

He found himself thinking about the last few days in this extraordinary setting. Each day seemed to have added something to his awakening self. From rock hard surfaces to the clumps of summer flowers that looked like shooting stars, to the painfully cold rivulets breaking free from the snowfields Twang had found himself being affected by this landscape. It was not something he could articulate yet. His sketches had captured views, quick views of places he had felt in his eyes and on his short hikes around the lake but they did not capture the effects of the clear crisp air he woke up to or the sounds of the wind wafting through the high fir trees or the feel of the clear cold water on his face.

Today, in this early morning solitude he was going to take his clothes off and walk the rock-strewn path to Blue Lake. It was as if he had 6 days of preparation. Six days to really break from the last 18 years, and here,

here, he had found the openness to look at his life differently. Somehow he wanted to consecrate that change. That is when he started his walk to Blue Lake. The sun was still shooting streaks of light through the rocky tors, the wind seemed to bring silence. He stopped. Ahead of him, facing him was a blue tailed lizard. It might as well have been a mythical beast from another time. His heart quickened. This was not the first lizard he had seen here but today it seemed different. Here, facing him today was something out of his childhood memories. Memories of his nanny's stories when he was growing up. Stories of Knights of Old fighting dragons, particularly St. George. They were usually the final test of a knight's courage. What was he to make of this lizard, this dragon poised and waiting for him. He stood there in his nakedness while his senses turned themselves into a kind of vibration. His childhood fears of dragons and trolls and darkness seemed to melt under the focus of his being. Here was the path he had found. Here he was going to go forward. He stepped forward and walked with a feeling of lightness and focus that he couldn't remember having had before. The blue tailed lizard disappeared as fast as it had come into his focus. He walked on to Blue Lake and when he got to the water he walked in letting the cold snow fed water envelope him. He walked on until he was totally immersed. His body felt like it was going to die it was so cold yet he stayed in until he no longer felt the water and he swam in exuberance. When he finally emerged from this watery awakening he knew he was no longer the child who had come here not too many days ago.

In his heightened sense of awareness he walked back to his tent, put on his clothes, took his sketchbook and walked towards the eastern side of the mountain until he found a view looking down. He set himself up with his paper and his pastels. He looked with new eyes. He looked for signs and patterns. He looked for deeper inner patterns. In this way he scanned the land below him, until it seemed like something was forming out of the rocks strewn about. He kept focusing until he could make out what looked like a broken down cabin, an old structure with the roof caved in. He had not seen it before. Now, he would try and capture it on paper.

T-Rex

Big Ben had come early to Betsy's this morning.. He had stopped by there every day since he noticed the T-Rex signature in the Forest Service's sign in book. He knew it was Twangly's because he had seen him spray paint that signature on some walls when he was younger. That was Twangly's...that was the moniker he used for some very interesting artwork he had spray painted on someone else's wall. Ben had not told his mother or father about Twangly's "art work" and it turned out he didn't have to. One close call with a bookstore owner running after him was enough to keep Twangly's images in his sketchbook. Since those wild years T-Rex had not been seen by Ben until he looked at the register. At least he could report to his colleagues at the estate that he knew where Twang was and by all indications he was safe, that he was backpacking in the mountains. He told them he would hang out at a local cafe, stay in Winthrop and wait until things change.

This morning he came early. He wasn't sure why. He couldn't sleep any longer. Now he was checking his messages. Nothing. He looked at the global positioner. Two blips were within 15 miles of where he sat. He knew Twangly was one of them, about 15 miles north of Masama if he had gone to Blue Lake. The other was about 15 miles south of Masama. It was still as perplexing as ever but he had let it go because, well, because . . .

"What are you playing this morning?" Betsy asked him. She had seen him enough times playing solitaire on the screen. This morning she saw the map and the two blips.

"Ah, it's a geography game," he simply answered not wanting to bring any more attention to what he was doing.

"Are you tired of solitaire?" she asked.

"Actually I do like company at times," he told her.

"Clever," she answered back. She kind of liked him and had fun with his accent.

"Oh, oh, here they come," she whispered to him.

"Here who comes?"

"Oh, the swat team, our resident camouflaged guys, fat and lean I call them. Isn't it amazing how they blend in."

Ben shielded the newspaper in front of him

"Who are they?"

"I don't know. They've been coming in. I think they are staying in a cabin here."

She went over. "What'll it be, Gents? Toast and cereal again, with tea?"

They just nodded.

Ben eyed them from the side of the paper. "Fat and lean," he thought, "that fits them to a tee but there's something else that fits them." He just shook his head in disbelief as his memory was jolted and brought back the past. "All these years," he began, "all these years and those two haven't changed. How could they. They were a comic duo then and they looked like one now. If they weren't so brutally tragic they could have been a comedy team. But the revolution made them into zealots and now they are here, in Masama. After all these years. Can they really think that Twang still matters, that he warrants being assassinated? Can they really think that they will get away with that, let alone get any money for him?"

He slid further down in his seat. "They must know that Twang is here. They're waiting for him to come back or they're going to find him. If they're going to attempt to kill him then the mountains would be a perfect place. This may be our final reckoning, after all these years."

Road to Destiny

Mariah stood up and practically shouted, "we've got to get moving. Come on, Jim, let's take this young man out to meet his destiny."

They took Twing by the arms and started him out the front door.

"Wait a minute," Twing implored, "I know you won't like this, Mariah, but I'd like to take the jeep over to the trailhead. I'd like to try her out. I'll park away from you so you won't see it."

Mariah just gently asked him, "do you know where the trailhead is, Twing?"

"Yes, I can find it. Don't worry, I'll meet you there."

Mariah got into Jim's pickup and drove down the farm road to Highway 20. Twing went back into his room, grabbed his coat and out of a zippered pocket took out the pouch that his mother had given him, opened it up and got out the ring. He had kept it in the pouch since he started working on the farm. He had looked at it on several other occasions but this time he put it on. He felt like it was the thing to do. He imagined it had a connection to some ancient power. It was beautiful. It must be, must be made of pure inlaid gold with different gems or jewels that formed the tail of a peacock. He could not tell what the peacock was made of, a dark crystal or something. This was one time he would wear it.

He left his coat, grabbed the keys and ran out to Evermore. She needed a new life but the image of the comet on the side would remain. He drove to the trailhead and saw the pickup parked close to the trail. He drove as far down the lot as he could to park the jeep. He ran to them. They had gone up the trail, to a map of the Blue Lake area.

"We're finally on our way," drawled Jim.

"It's about time, don't you think, Twing? Mariah looked at him.

Fat and Lean

The radicals took their time eating breakfast. It gave Ben the chance to check his screen once again. The map emerged and the two blips came on. He noticed the one from Winthrop moving north, getting closer to the other one. He was still perplexed but excited about some activity.

"Two rings," he thought, "it can't be." He sat waiting for them in his car until the unmistakable duo came out of Betsy's, falling over each other. "What is the matter with you?" Radical 2 berated his sidekick. In an agitated voice Radical 26 answered back, "We didn't have to break in, did we? I mean, they are going to find out..."

"Relax, we won't be here, and they won't find out until he checks out."

"Which could be anytime."

"Anytime, will be no time."

"What do you mean, no time?"

"We are going to check him out and this time there will be nothing but his birthmark left behind, which we will need, along with the ring, to collect the money."

Radical 26 grimaced as they hopped into a white van and sped off.

Ben followed them at a safe distance. They came to the parking lot of the Blue Lake trailhead. He passed by them. After five minutes or so he turned around and drove into the parking lot. By this time he noticed their van, a pickup truck and a jeep at the end of the lot. He got out and slowly started up the trail.

Great-Granddaddies Cabin

Twang's pastels caught the sun just as it lit up the inside of the cabin. "This is as close as I'll get to Glastonbury," he thought, "the sun shines on both of these." He held his golden chalk, drove it across the paper again and again until a presence of shadows, moving contrasts destroyed his moment of epiphany. "Someone has come into my sanctuary," he thought as he glared into the brightness. He could not pull himself away.

Jim was the first to find the ruins of the cabin. Like finding an image in a puzzle, he discerned the ruins from the rocks and logs strewn about.

"Jim, this is amazing. It looks like my painting. I mean, this is old, this is . . . It's your great great-grandfather who built this, isn't it?"

She walked inside with Twing behind her. She was too over come to finish her sentence.

"Be careful," Jim cautioned them. The roof beams only fell a few years ago. This is not earthquake proof or rockslide proof.

Mariah fell on her knees, "Jim, look over here, under this beam."

They all looked. It was a bone sticking out of the dirt. She started to dig with her fingers. Twing helped move the sticks and tried to move the large old beam over it. She kept digging and more bones came into view. She felt the roundness of a skull.

"This is a human" she cried out, "we found the bones of someone."

"They must have gotten hit by this beam," Jim offered.

Mariah dug some more. She didn't want to. She was impelled to. She dug out the skull. She thought, "it can't be." She felt a small hard sharp object in the dirt. She picked it up, knowing, fearing, hoping it would not be what she thought. She slowly spread open her hand. There, in its sharp fiery outline was what looked like a pendant. She scraped the dirt off. It was a comet, an earring, his earring, only his earring. She had found him. She had found her love, her comet. A man who came as close to her as any man had ever come. She had found him, here in the ruins of an old cabin. What could she say. She was overcome. Jim just stood by Twing. They could not say anything. Her tears were flowing like a trail of moonlight . . .

Birthmarks

By now Twang was on his way towards the cabin. He, too was drawn to it. He carefully worked his way over the rocks and towards it when someone called out.

"You there?"

Twang stopped to look. On the trail stood two men in camouflage clothes. A tall one and a short fatter one.

"Yes," Twang said.

"Hold it right there," the tall one ordered.

When Twang looked at him he could see the man had a gun in his hand.

"What do you want?" Twang asked.

"Stay right there," the tall one ordered. "Go tie his hands," he told the shorter one. Radical 26 walked over to Twang when out of the ruins of the old cabin walked Twing who had heard the voices. Twing's hat was off and he had his T-shirt on. He looked out at the young man who had no shirt on. He saw the two men. He saw the gun. He looked again at the young man. He looked and Twang looked. They saw each other's faces. They saw the birthmarks on their necks. Twing knew who he had found. Twang was not sure where he was or what was happening. Here was his double.

Radical 2 blinked his eyes. Radical 26 looked back and forth at the two young men.

Out of nowhere came a voice.

"So you've finally caught up with him." It was Big Ben sounding like the midnight tolling of the bells.

Radical 2 turned around. He eyed the short man with a mustache. He knew the voice. He fired a shot. Big Ben was hit in the arm. Now it was Twing's turn. All the hours of throwing and paring and sensing the flow of an opponent was focused in him now. He turned and turned into Radical 2, grabbed his gun hand and as Radical 2 turned to grab Twing, Twing used the movement to throw him over. As soon as his feet were off the ground there was nothing Radical 2 could do. Twing flung him forward and he landed on some rocks. Twing went for his gun but there was no movement from Radical 2. Radical 26 tried to pull his gun out but it was too late. Big Ben shot him twice but only manage to wound him in the leg. Radical 26 fell down writhing in pain. His face showed the fear that comes with the possibility of death. He began to cry. He begged for mercy. He had no intention of harming Twang. He never had. He was just going along with Radical 2, just following orders, coerced by Radical 2.

"A strike!" Lightning Bill thought he saw a strike on this day of intense sunlight. He looked up the peak on his map. It was near Blue Lake. But there was no smoke. It couldn't be. I thought I saw a strike near Blue Lake. It's the most incredible thing. There is not a cloud in the sky.

They all heard it. They all felt it. It seemed to crack open the mountain. The mountain began to tremble, began to rumble, like pebbles trickling down a cliff, then with rocks and dust and more rocks moving and destroying everything in its path.

Jim was the first to yell out, "it's a rock slide, a landslide, run, run."

Twing and Twang and Mariah started running past the cabin. Then Jim came but could not keep up.

"Go without me, go!" he yelled.

But Twing and Twang wanted to go back until they saw a large rock come out of nowhere and hit Jim. Mariah screamed, "He's hit! He's hit!, run boys, please run". All three of them ran until there was no breath left in them.

The rockslide continued on behind them. Big Ben had run the other way. When the noise finally stopped they looked over. The dust and dirt and trees and rocks had covered everything and everywhere they had stood an eternity ago. The ruins of the cabin were gone. The tall man and they presumed the short man, his sidekick, had perished in the rock fall. Jim was nowhere to be seen. Half the mountain seemed to have buried them.

"Is anyone there?" They heard a voice from across the rocks. It was Big Ben.

"Yes, yes, we are, we are here," shouted Mariah.

They climbed over and found Big Ben still bleeding from the wound on his arm.

"Here, let me put something around that," she said, and was going to rip up her shirt when Twing offered his T-shirt.

Mountain Grace

They did not know what to say. They all looked over the landslide. "It must be 20 to 30 feet high," someone said.

"What a grave this turned out to be." Big Ben answered, as they let the silence descend on them.

Twing slowly looked around trying to make eye contact with Twang and said with an emotional voice, "What a way to meet my brother."

They all finally climbed back up to Twang's camp and helped him pack up. In an eerie yet solemn procession they slowly walked down the trail. Each still

124

pondering what had happened in this tragic and miraculous event. Mariah finally opened up their private reveries.

"Jim Bridger found my future soul mate, my husband and I, years ago stranded on a mountain pass. Over the years he was our rock to build on. Now he has become part of the very rocks of the mountains he lived on, Jim, Jim, you showed us the way. Who would have thought that my Comet would die here in the very cabin that you lived in and that we would . . ." she was half crying, half gushing, like a geyser that blows every ten years a so, "that we would, that we would find him on the very day two brothers, two twin brothers would see each other again for the very first time."

"Comet, you were telling me all along where you were only I didn't see it in my paintings until Jim looked. He saw it. He saw the cabin and it was to become his dying place."

"I, too, find this meeting an extraordinary event," Big Ben added to the conversation in his accented voice. "I have been your shadow, Twang, over all these many years. I can tell you stories of your life that read like a photograph book. I'm not sure you knew me but I think you may have seen me. It's just never occurred to you that I was employed by your father to be a kind of guardian. Not that I could really do too much but he trusted me. We had been through the turbulent times together and I stayed loyal to him and your mother. I became part of the family and your growing up. I took an interest in your welfare so your father asked me to watch over you because of his business and political relationships."

Twing was by now almost beside himself with questions. He walked behind Twang, walked beside Twang, walked in front of him and just kind of shook his head in amazement. He finally just yelled in exuberance, "I have a brother." They all turned around and Twang looked at him and they held each other and hugged each other, there, on the trail away from Blue Lake on the side of a mountain in the northwest of America. Two very different souls and upbringings meeting after 18 years.

"Where do we start, Master Twing?" Twang asked him.

"I guess we start right here, Twang. I left Boulder Creek, California when I read this impossible, improbable letter from two people who came to the cafe I worked at."

"What did they look like?" Twang and Big Ben asked, almost together. When Twing told them, Beg Ben postulated that it was Dr. Highshe and his nurse Camec, who had also left the estate in England a week before

Twang. "From what I know," Big Ben stated, "they were going to take a trip to the western states of America. It is quite possible that they left you the letter in Boulder Creek, California, but I had no idea that Twang had a brother, let alone a twin brother."

"How could your father and mother not tell me," he wondered out loud, "it is a mystery that is maybe not the only mystery here. There may be things I do not know but I think I found the answer to a very perplexing problem."

"You have a ring, Twang, that your father or mother gave you on your journey to this land. This ring emits a pulse that I can pick up on a geographic screen, a kind of global positioner. The position of this ring became a blip on the screen. I followed your blip from Seattle but then a second blip came on the screen, which also became apparent at Seattle, but this one went south through Wenatchee and then came north.

As he was saying this, Twing held up his hand and showed them all the ring on his finger. They took a closer look and Twang said it was just like his. "The rings of Urum!" Big Ben stated in a solid voice. "They are as old as the oldest kingdoms in Asia. This explains the two blips. You and Twang both have one. But how did you get it?" he asked Twing.

"My mother gave to me before I left. She said, "it was

a gift from my father."

"And who is your father?" Mariah asked him.

It was a question Twing had wanted to ask himself but was terribly afraid of finding out.

"Who is my real father? Twing asked Twang.

Twang was not sure what to say. He never had to share his father before. He had lived as the only child.

"I, ah, I, you'll have to meet him. They, he, never mentioned you. No one ever did. Now that you're here . . . incredible! a twin brother! We may have to change our names. Twing and Twang is a bit much. How about Remus and Romulus. We could start our own empire."

"I don't know about empires," Twing said, "but we can start as brothers and go from here. That is, unless there are other camouflaged swat teams who want to do away with you or me. I don't know who they were and what they have to do with you. There were definitely surprised when I walked out of the old cabin."

Big Ben again elucidated the conversation, "I don't know that we'll see any more of these kind, at least not here. They were left over revolutionaries. I knew them before the overthrow. They became part of the assassination team.

"What do we have to do with them?" Twing and Twang both asked at the same time.

128

"Your father," he let the sound reverberate into all of them. "Your father," he said as solemnly and as stately as he could, "was the king of Perseus and your mother was the queen,"

"Twang turned his head very slowly. He thought his father had political and business connections but with his mouth wide-open he showed that he had not known the whole story. Twing could only look in amazement and disbelief. Mariah was dumb struck.

Big Ben told him that when their royal family was exiled, shortly after they were born, they left with nothing from the palace except what they could carry. The rings were part of a small treasure they took.

"But why was I sent away for adoption?" asked Twing.

Ben could only guess, "I myself, did not know there were two boys. I can only think that they were afraid of two children in danger of being assassinated. You see the Radicals put a price on the head of the heir. That was you, Twang. It was just that, it was relatively safe in England. That is why I have been your guardian all these years and why your father insisted that you could not travel out of England. But, again, there are two people who might know."

"Who?" asked Twing.

"The queen's doctor, Dr. Highshe and his nurse

Camec. The same ones who most likely gave you the letter. They also have been loyal to the royal family and they were with the queen when you were born Twang and now, I would assume, who were with you when you were born, Twing. It makes sense that it was them. They would know," Ben continued, "I just didn't know they were going to find or make contact with a long lost heir to the throne when they left for America. I've been in touch with them over the years but as I've found out several times I don't know everything. You, Twing are as much news to me as you are to Twang."

Before any of them expected it, they were at the trailhead. Mariah said, "We have a lot to work out. I'll get a hold of Sheriff O'Malley. It's probably best that we don't advertise this."

"Yes," said Ben, "I would prefer to stay out of the media. For the two boys, the safest approach would be for them to also stay out of the media. Is it possible that you, Mariah, could tell the sheriff that you were with Jim when the landslide came. He is gone and you, you live."

Mariah agreed with them, "but Ben, you'll have to go to a doctor with me. After that we will all meet at the farm."

Twing told Twang that he had a Jeep for them to ride in on the drive home.

"It's an old army jeep that I just tuned up. It was Comet's Jeep, Mariah's husband, and she doesn't want to see it."

She heard this and told him, "that time is over with, Twing. Comet had disappeared and today I found him as I never would have imagined and now he's with an old friend who brought me to him. I found his bones and I have his earring. I have all the good memories of our life together without the nagging ache of what happened to him. Please ride that Jeep and put some new adventures on."

"Can we take your car?" she asked Ben, "I don't have the keys to Jim's truck."

As they drove away and headed south they passed the Forest Service Rangers driving towards the Blue Lake trailhead. They will find an old pickup truck and a white van in the parking lot. A convergence of stars, planets, local weather and a few loud gunshots had brought them to a climax of changes. The fear of death did not save Radical 26 nor did the fanatical habits of Radical 2. Jim Bridger had died as he had lived. He was a constant force for all who met him, part history, part land as powerful as the rock that laid him in his grave. What would they do with his pickup when they find it. Put it out to pasture like his horse along with his buckskin coat and his coonskin hat?

For Big Ben it was the end of the revolution, the last act of the turbulent times. Now he could let go. Yes, he did have some questions for the king and queen but he was content to try and contact his colleagues in the household at the estate. If he could find out where the doctor or Camec were, that would be enough. He could ask them how the brothers got separated. But at this point, it was only out of curiosity. He had other ideas. He would stop in to see Betsy, maybe hangout some more, play solitaire together.

Twing put on his hat and Twang threw his backpack in the back of the jeep. "There is a comet on the side but I've christened her 'Evermore'," Twing told him. "She's got a few more miles in her and I think we, you and I, can put a few more on." The time for recalling the past, their lives up till now, could wait. They were feeling the vibrations of 100 horses under the hood, they were open to the wind. Twing held onto his hat, Twang held onto his seat. Man, they were feeling it.

"Where are we going to?" Twang asked.

"Where ever we want to." Twing told him with all the assurance of eternal youth.

The Soothsayer's Rantings

When they finally did get back to Twang's cabin at Masama it was a frustrating yet almost inevitable end for the young man who was to have become king. His cabin had been ransacked and the one thing he wanted to find was gone. "The ring is gone!" he shouted. "Here's the pouch, empty. They took the ring. Those leftover maniacs took my ring. It's buried under half a mountain of rock along with them."

This was just another one of those reminders that seem to exemplify fragile mortality but like children in a sandbox it did not deter them very long from continuing in their exhilaration. Twang had a lifetime to makeup for the loss of a gold ring, besides it hadn't really changed anything. Twing had the peacock ring, the reminder of an ancient empire but at that moment neither realized that it was on the hand that tradition would have placed it on. In a tragic irony the soothsayer's future was becoming their future.

"Why don't you stay at Mariah's with me?" Twing asked him.

"I've got this room for the summer," Twang added, "but I don't have to stay here. We can use the cabin if we do anymore hiking or my friend Rushdie could stay here. That's one person I want to call. He won't believe this, in fact, I don't know of anyone who will believe this. We have to figure out what to do, how to . . ." He became flustered.

"I don't think I want to hurry that," Twing said, "I'm going to call my mother in Boulder Creek. I'm sure she's been worrying about me. Do you know that tomorrow is July 4th? Fireworks day. It's actually Independence Day. I think we've got something to celebrate about."

"You mean our own independence?" Twang said, "I'm breaking away from England again, a very old empire"

"I'm actually reconnecting to a past I didn't know about, but I don't feel its weight. I've got the West in me and it looks like we are both ready to celebrate."

Angelina's Tears

"Angelina is coming, boys." Mariah sang out to them, "and is she going to be surprised. I mean she knows about Twing but she knows nothing about Twang. Two handsome young men." She looked at both of them and then whispered, "the sons of a king."

Twang took this as his cue and he became Malcolm, a Prince of Denmark who stood up:

> "With this there grows
> In my most ill-composed affection such
> A stanchless avarice that, were I king,

I should cut off the nobles for their lands,
Desire his jewels and this other's house:
And my more-having would be as a sauce
To make me hunger more"

Maria looked on in amazement wondering what he was talking about and Twing, no stranger to performing took his cue from the country songs he'd heard as he grew up in Boulder Creek. He grabbed Mariah's guitar and started a stately rhythm,

"From a jack to a king, la da da da . . .,

Malcolm came back and ironically articulated their day:

Nay, had I power, I should
Pour the sweet milk of concord into hell,
Uproar the universal peace, confound
All unity on earth.

"I think it is now a night of harmony that we want, Prince Twang, after all this uproar and turbulence," at which Twing began singing a new song from an ancient book,

To everything, turn, turn, turn, there is a
season, turn, turn, turn, and a time for
every purpose under heaven.

As they were reconciling their royal future, Mariah put on an
old tie-died scarf over her head, grabbed a buckskin vest and
now she was the exotic western cowboy Princess these two
Prince's were trying to attract. They reacted with exuberance
and they all rid themselves of the trauma of a few hours ago as
they joined Twing in the chorus,

To everything, turn, turn, turn,
There is a season, turn, turn, turn,
And a time for every purpose under heaven.

It was, it was a play within a grand moment. It was a
remembrance of what could be in a childhood world. It
was an exuberance of youth and infectious joy. It was a
door opening, a door opening, the front door opening
with the afternoon light outlining a figure, a youthful
figure, a child woman with tight golden brown dread
lock curls flowing like wild ferns around a beautifully
defined face. A tall slim figure dressed in a white dress
with a colored sash and cowboy boots. Within this space,
within this time the soft sound of a faraway song
breathed into them,

"There's a brown girl in the light,
Tra la la la la
There's a brown girl in the light,
Tra la la la la la
"There's a brown girl in the light,
Tra la la la la
She is heaven, while my heart takes flight.

It was music that might have been as everything changed in the room. Mariah slowly sat down and the princess and princes moved in slow motion.

"There's a brown girl in the light . . .

"Angelina" Mariah finally called out. Angelina never sounded so appropriate. A soft and earthly angel if ever there was one. "This is Twing, Mariah said and this, this is his long-lost twin brother Twang."

They just looked. Angelina looked. They weren't sure what to say.

"Hi," they all said at once. Now they laughed and their laughter broke the silence even more. They smiled and laughed again.

"Twing and Twang," Angelina said, "how did you get those names?"

"They are the sons of a king." Mariah chimed in.

"Let's drop that," Twang said. "yea, we're just the Blue Lake boys," Twing offered with a sly grin while looking at Twang and then Angelina.

"Actually, Masama, is the rebirth of these two. They found each other here and they didn't die on the mountain like . . ." Mariah didn't mean to say it but it started to come out. It was the bitter to the sweet and Mariah could not help but tell Angelina that Jim died on the mountain. "There is more than that, my angel. We found that, that is, Jim help me find the bones of your father."

Angelina's face lost color and she wanted to sit down.

"How do you know?" she asked.

Mariah took out the comet earring she had found next to the skull. Angelina took it in her hand, held it and just looked at it. "My daddy," she whispered, while tears crept down her cheek.

"Tears never crept so beautifully on such a cheek," thought Twang.

"Brown eyes crying in the rain," thought Twing.

They let the time pass slowly until Mariah spoke, "Let's not be too sad. We found your father and your godfather found him. It was as if your father called him home. Jim lived on the land and your father came from, well, you know, I was never really sure from where.

They are buried up there with two misfits who finally found a resting place for their discontented life."

"What happened there? I heard about a landslide in the news. This all sounds quite incredible. How did you find each other?" Angelina was now engrossed in the story. She looked at both Twing and Twang. Twing started by telling her how he received the letter from two strangers while he was working in Boulder Creek. The stories went on and on, from Twing to Twang to Mariah to Twing again and Twang again until Mariah brought out tea and they finally just took a walk out on the farm to see the horses and give Angelina a view of the restored jeep.

"I call her 'Evermore'," Twing said.

They all heard a caw from a nearby branch.

"That raven's been with me ever since I started to work on it," Twing told them.

"I gave it to Twing," Mariah said, "for him to fix up and keep. He's been helping me a lot and I haven't had the money to pay him."

Before they came back from their walk, Mariah suggested that all three of them go for ride in the jeep and check on Big Ben at the Oregon Trail Motel.

"He may be at Betsy's cafe, though," she said, "I think he's found someone to play solitaire with. Tonight, we'll all go to the Winthrop drive-in for the fireworks."

Sheriff O'Malley

Before she could turn around all three of them had hopped into Evermore. Twing was gunning the engine. They left some dust as Mariah called out, "be careful".

They drove past the Pearrygin Lake parking lot. There was an empty space where a white van used to park. They drove left onto Highway 20 and on into Winthrop. First they stopped at the Oregon Trail Motel and knocked on room No. 12. No one answered. They drove on into town, which was already filled with visitors for the fireworks later that night. Traffic was stop and go and they were following the cars when an old Chevy sedan pulled in front of them from a side street. They could not help but bump into its bumper as Twing skidded to a quick stop. The sedan stopped and out of the driver's side came a burly, bearded giant, his face red with anger and yelling, "Whaddeya think you're doin messing with the Browser." From the other side came a mousy looking guy with a big cowboy hat Twing recognized as the kid who took his backpack.

There were already some honking cars behind them as this burly Browser came up to Twing. But this time Twing was ready for him. "These are the guys who took my backpack!" Twing yelled to Twang and Angelina. The Browser came up to Twing and was ready to punch him when Twing's training in Aikido came through. Browser threw a punch and Twing moved lightning fast, grabbing Browser's fist and shoving it into the rear view mirror, scraping a few knuckles and crushing the mirror.

Browser just roared. Cars started honking louder. A siren could be heard. Twing grabbed Browser's head in a headlock. The squeaky mouse came out on the other side of the jeep and Angelina gave him a good kick in the chest. The cars honked louder, the siren came closer and stopped next to them. Sheriff O'Malley got out.

"Hold it, hold it, hold it" the Sheriff said, as he came up behind Browser and pushed his left arm behind him.

Browser backed up with the Sheriff and Twing and Twang holding him. Angelina got out and gave mouse another push.

Browser was finally subdued. Sheriff O'Malley asked him what happened? They all started talking.

"Hold it, hold it, hold it," the Sheriff yelled again.

"You, what's your name?"

"Twing."

"And yours?"

"Twang"

"They drove into my car!" Browser could hardly hold himself.

"They pulled right in front of us. We could not avoid them. I was lucky to only bump his bumper."

"Is that right? Mr. . . . Mr . . ."

"Browser. They smashed into us"

"You pulled in front of us."

"All right Twing," said the Sheriff.

"No, I'm Twang, he's Twing."

"And who is this?"

"That's Angelina,"

Mouse squeaked, "We were just following traffic when this guy came barreling down on us"

"That's a lie!" Angelina said. "You pulled in front of us."

The honking was getting out of hand.

"Shnauser," the Sheriff said in a perturbed voice.

"That's Browser, O'Malley."

"Sheriff O'Malley to you, son, Sheriff O'Malley!" looking up to the burly giant and pointing his finger at his chest.

Twing finally said, "These are the two guys who took my backpack a few weeks ago."

"What you talking about?" squeaked the mouse.

"Look in their trunk," said Twing.

"Pull over to the curb, Shnauser and you, Squeaky, stay here."

"That's Browser not Shnauser, O'Malley.

"That's Sheriff O'Malley, son, Sheriff O'Malley."

"And it's not squeaky it's Mouse."

"Move it Twang."

"I'm Twing not Twang."

"Twing, Twang, walla, walla, bing, bang," a bystander added to the confusion. This last addition broke them all up into bouts of surreal laughter.

"Good God, get off the road, all of you," the sheriff could hardly contain himself.

The honking had grown deafening. The Chevy sedan moved over. The jeep followed. The cars moved down the Main Street. The honking stopped. The Sheriff told Browser to open up the trunk.

Browser got his keys and opened the trunk. Inside

was the backpack, still intact with Twing's clothes.

"That's my backpack." Twing said, "thank you for not dumping it."

Twing looked at the Sheriff and said, "Look, we bumped his car, he took my backpack. If he pays for my mirror I'm willing to forget it."

The Sheriff looked at Browser and said, "I think you're damned lucky here. I think both you and squeaky . . .

"That's Mouse, Sheriff."

"All right, all right, both of you owe this young man an apology."

Browser and Mouse looked at each other and held out their hands to Twing.

"That was a damn mean trick to pull on you," Browser told Twing.

"I'm sorry about that," the Mouse said.

They all kind of looked at the at each other, the Sheriff looked at them when the angel voice said, "then I think it's time we started celebrating the 4th, don't you think."

The Fourth of July

They all high-fived it, even the Browser, and thanked
the Sheriff, got the backpack, hopped in their Jeep,
hopped in their car and drove into the celebration.
When they finally picked up Mariah, Big Ben was there
with Betsy.

"Betsy told them Ben had never celebrated the 4th of
July before. I'm going to take him."

"I don't think Twang has either. We're going to take
him," said Twing.

Before they rode out to the Winthrop drive-in they
replayed their weird and wild odyssey with Browser and
Mouse and Sheriff O'Malley while Mariah and Big Ben
and Betsy laughed until they cried. This hilarious tale
had the affects of floodgates opening, allowing them to

drown in the last day's events with pain and laughter. When they finally got on the road it seemed like the whole county was going to the Winthrop drive-in and this had all been a part of an American panorama including the bumper cars. They stood in line for the grilled hot dogs and corn on the cob, caramel apples and apple cider and had a grand old American feast while waiting for the fireworks to start.

It was unlike any fireworks they had ever experienced. It was as if the stars burst. Shower after shower of starlight cascaded down while they waited for the next explosion until finally the finale came and brought with it what looked like a comet, shooting star light in the shape of a comet, from the direction of Blue Lake glowing, flowing, bursting through the darkness. They looked at it and they could see an old cowboy riding on its tail, hanging on for all he was worth. Oh, it was a night to remember, and they would not be the same ever again.

Epilogue

Somewhere there's always a convergence of events, or more specifically a convergence of human events. People, through their dreams and their waking consciousness take part in a miraculous unfolding. They live within the past and the past is a cosmic journey. They live with innate hopes of a future. Somewhere in between the past and the future our lives take place.

Was Captain Ahab acting out inevitable events begun eons ago? Was his First Mate? Were they destined to die in that historic encounter with the whale with one-man left to tell the story. Did Joseph Smith see God and his son in a grove of trees? Did they tell him where golden books were hidden? Did Mohammed wrestle with the angel? Did Gabriel visit him in his dreams? Did the future come out of this wrestling in the sand? And what about the sand covering ancient seas and prehistoric life. It has all metamorphosed into oil, into economic power in this meeting of past and future.

It was late and the Doctor was musing again. His writings had brought him some moments of peace. He knew they were simply metaphysical ramblings but it was not the questioning of his writings he was after, it was simply the doing, the doing. Especially after all these years of inactivity, of hoping for a different future.

148

It was all too late, his time was counted in what he had done, in what he had kept with him. He had been loyal to his friend the King. As he looked back their minuscule acts filled him with warmth. Yes, warmth, and he thought, "this is what life turns out to be, moments of remembrances, some of which add to what it means to be human, in our potential, in our beatitude, in our grace, in our destiny.

Dr. Highshe had kept the secret for too many years. Camec, his companion, for as many years, had stayed with him. Their mutual understanding of historic events had brought them together and kept them together. Like a geological layer their moment of secret experience had been laid down 18 years ago. Two children were born to the Queen that day, the first to sit on the Peacock throne, the other to watch and wait.

He had kept the soothsayers words in mind as the years had covered the layer of secrets. "If I sliced through these layers, these years," he thought, "I could see my life, all there." The year of secrets was now embedded under the weight of history and through it, and through it he saw their life." His contemplation was interspersed with his writing. He had begun to write his memoirs and it was like slicing through layers of events. Some laid in turbulence, some in lightness. "It seemed so appropriate," he thought, "to begin his memoirs with this analogy. It had occurred to him as they traveled up the western coast of America along Highway 1. Occasionally, he had seen these layers of sediment showing through the side of the highway, where the road builders had cut through a hillside. Sometimes, the lines were up and almost vertical. Sometimes the lines undulated until they fell into the Pacific.

As they traveled north along this edge of land and sea he felt a time of his life ending, a layer of events being covered by the beginning of acceptance. On that edge he had felt the need to carry out reconciliation. He would find the long abandoned Twingly and let him know about his brother. After 18 years he felt this need to rectify what had been set in motion at their birth.

"His loyalty to his friend the King would technically be kept," he thought, "because he had never sworn to keep his secret from Twingly. It was Twangly who had been brought up in England with his mother and father in relative normality, at least in terms of English aristocratic normality with money and an estate and the best schools.

It was Twingly who was lost and grew up in a new world. It was time to rectify this, to set this in motion. Just as his life had taken its own turns, he now felt turned to this.

Big Sur was unlike anything he had seen along the

coast of England. A western edge of hills, fir trees and cliffs falling into the sea, shrouded in early-morning mist and fog. Camec held him and caressed his face while they watched the light soften the mist. "It had come to this," he thought, "All these years of secrets and frustrations had come to an ethereal world on this western edge of land. We were still together and, ironically, may not have been so if we had stayed in the old country with a revolutionary government. No, it was a decision, one of those decisions that you look back on and wonder. If we had stayed, we probably would not be here right now,. We also might have been involved in building a different society. If we had stayed. What was right in our choice. We grew together over the years couched in our trauma of the revolution and in our secrets with the King and his family."

Now the mist was rising, light was breaking over the hills above them. He had packed the car and they were ready to set off on their destined path. What a beautiful setting it was. They were going further north to a place called Boulder Creek. It was there they had the last knowledge of Twingly and his family.

I don't think I want to leave them just yet. They are traveling north on Highway 1, the coast highway. It was built when California was a fabled land, fraught with a history of genocide and opportunity. It's beauty and possibility seemed incomparable. Where there was desert there was growth. The land was fertile. Here, along the coast, the forests of redwoods grew and minds were open to possibilities that could only come from t his abundance, this mixture, this combination of beauty and potential.

It was along the Big Sur coast they stopped at a place called Esalen. It was a center for the "human potential" movement where another kind of cultural evolution was being waged. Isolated and subtle, it seemed an exploration of what it means to be human without the dogmas, the holy books, the fundamentalist's narrow views or the tyrant's power. It was, however, not formed enough for the doctor and Camec, but it did leave them with a lingering feeling, with a touch of a long lost Eden.

They had sat in the hot pools over looking the Pacific Ocean as the sun set. The sounds of the surf crashing on the rocks below was dramatic to them. It was almost like the sea could not stand for them (maybe for all who were at this place) to feel too complacent, too enthralled. The sea was reminding them that all sensual beauty was eventually going to crash down upon them, to continually be crushed. Even idealistic intent for cultural change was constantly being crushed. This was the message of the sea.

Now they were coming into the Monterey Bay Area

and the Carmel mission. Here they stopped to walk around. It was a tourist stop but they were also visitors. They were young lovers visiting and traveling in a new world. After the years of disappointments and frustrated dreams they walked together and stopped to look at the carved statutes outside the chapel. A wooden Christ on a cross. His agony was accentuated by the decaying wood.

"How could people worship this image of pain?" He wondered. "What did it mean to them?". While he was wondering he felt himself weak and told Camec he wanted sit down and just sit quietly for a while. Camec sensed his need and went to stroll through the gardens. Here, in this chapel, his life seemed to take on a new meaning. Even with the constant stream of tourists he felt stillness and immersed himself in the history and the sacrifice of those who built this church, willingly and unwillingly. Their blood was in the ground, their spirits hovered within and without the adobe and plaster and wooden beams and infused the images and statutes. These left over ideals of former revolutions. He was surrounded by their sacrifice sitting in the chapel created and built by their hands, their toil. A sanctuary built between the earth and the sky.

"We are so small in our permanence yet so large in our hopes and our dreams and our endeavors," he wrote in his notebook.

Camec touched him on the shoulder and he came out of his reverie. They walked out in silence and continued on their journey north. "He would set the stars in motion." he thought, as he mentally composed a note for the long-lost son of his friend the deposed King of the Peacock throne.

Until we meet again

Other words and art by the Author

Goodbye Bolinas we'll see you again – a heart-rending, mind-bending, love-sending novel of a turbulent and extraordinary time.

Available through lulu.com/RNeumann

Labyrinth a mythic journey - a novel of two brothers finding themselves while on a timeless journey – from the days of yore to the techno halls of innovation.

Published by Bookstand Books.
Contact: highwayone@earthlink.net

On the Wings of a Swan - an allegory of love transcending the everyday - with watercolor illustrations by the author.

Available through lulu.com/RNeumann

from Pigeon Point to Point Reyes - a book of pastels and haikus inspired by the California coast.

Available through Lulu.com/RNeumann

I Am Always With You! by **Marianne Neumann**
My mother's journal from 1938 to 1945. Translated by the author. A beautiful love story in the midst of war.

Available through highwayone@earthlink.net

Rainer Neumann's life is punctuated with the endings and beginnings of places, ideas, relationships and a variety of creative pursuits. Throughout these he has had an on-going interest in the structural environments of our culture.